Crime and Croissants

Susan Kiernan-Lewis

Other books by Susan Kiernan-Lewis

Parlez-vous Murder?
Accent on Murder
A Bad Éclair Day
Free Falling
Going Gone
Heading Home
Blind Sided
Rising Tides
Cold Comfort
Never Never
Wit's End
Dead On
Murder in the South of France
Murder à la Carte
Murder in Provence
Murder in Paris
Murder in Aix
Murder in Nice
Murder in the Latin Quarter
Murder in the Abbey
Murder in the Bistro
Murder in Cannes
Swept Away
Carried Away
Stolen Away
Reckless
Shameless
Breathless
Heartless
Clueless
Hopeless

Crime and Croissants

Book 2 of the
Stranded in Provence Mysteries

Susan Kiernan-Lewis

San Marco Press, Atlanta
Copyright 2017

1

Once More into the Fray

Whoever invented cobblestone streets obviously never wore kitten heels.

This thought ran through my mind every time I stepped outside my twelfth century apartment building in the French village where I now live. I probably should rethink my footwear choices accordingly but I'm determined not to go into the new apocalypse looking like a homeless person.

I exaggerate only slightly because the two old ladies, Madames Cazaly and Becque who are my building neighbors and self-imposed authority of what Jules—that's me—should and shouldn't wear are constantly telling me I'm overdressed.

Naturally I tell them that I doubt they're truly French. Can you imagine? In the land of the fashion capital of the world? Someone telling you to dress *down*?

Fortunately, the language barrier prevents any and all hurt feelings.

In any event I'm yet again wobbling my way down the street to Chabanel's single and only village bar, Bar á GoGo, to meet with my cheese-selling friend Katrine Pelletier for a French lesson.

I have to say in the five weeks since I landed in this medieval French village in the south of France things have not gotten any easier.

For one thing, most of our batteries have now worn out, all the shelves of the Casino grocery stores have long since been stripped bare, our candles are gone and what few are left are selling on the black market road that rings the village as if they were made of platinum, and I am officially sick of eating cheese—just about the only thing that's still in abundance these days. Mind you, I say that last complaint only at whisper level since such a statement is considered high treason in France, cheese being the demigod and the holy grail all in one over here.

"Jules!" Katrine waved to me from one of the café tables outside the bar.

This bar is truly the nastiest looking dive I'd ever seen. It has an abandoned-looking front with worn painted words that are unintelligible even to the French. I'm sure this place was serving grog to the Romans when it first opened and the service and the alcohol hasn't changed or improved since.

Katrine and I air-kissed cheeks before I sat down.

"You look flushed," Katrine said, signaling to the waiter to bring our *kirs*.

"How do people walk on these stupid roads?" I said, rubbing my heel, convinced I twisted my ankle on the last chunk of projecting mortar as I hurried down the home stretch to the village square.

Katrine answered me in French as the waiter brought our drinks.

"I have no idea what you said," I said.

"We do not wear dress shoes in Chabanel," Katrine said with a shrug, pointing to her own very sensible flats.

"All I packed were dress shoes."

That wasn't true of course but if I had my way it would be. I love shoes—especially Italian ones—and any opportunity to wear them. I had to admit that since the dirty bomb exploded over the Mediterranean the month before, those opportunities were becoming fewer and fewer.

Actually, those opportunities were virtually nonexistent in Chabanel even *before* the bomb dropped.

"You should go shopping," Katrine said in French.

I waved away her words. "Speak English. You want me to spend my last few euros—with no hope of getting any more *ever*—and go shopping for shoes? *Bonne idée*, Katrine!" I said sarcastically.

She corrected my pronunciation.

"I'm not sure why I bother trying to learn French," I said with a sigh. "I'm hopeless at it. Besides, you people have too many words."

"In fact we have much fewer than English."

"All the more reason why you should all speak English instead. We have the more complete language."

"And yet it is French that you will speak until the day you die."

"Jeez, you're a real mood lifter, Katrine."

"I just think you ought to start thinking of Chabanel as your home now."

"America is my *home.*"

"You do know your home is where your friends are, do you not?"

"No offense, Katrine, but I've known you about five minutes and I have dozens of friends back in Atlanta. Hundreds."

I have to say she was really starting to annoy me. Just because *her* life was a hash doesn't mean everyone else's is. I knew Katrine was unhappy and that her weekly outing with me was one of her rare escapes from three small children and a largely clueless husband.

"*Si tu dis*," she said with a shrug before leaning over and whispering loudly, "Do not turn around, but there goes Chief DeBray. He's so handsome. And he's looking this way!"

I forced myself not to turn around. I hadn't seen much of Luc in the last few weeks and assumed it was because he'd either tired of my relentless neediness—I always had a problem these days—or he simply had his hands full trying to keep the village from going to wrack and ruin during the apocalypse.

I'm sure I wasn't the only one running out of supplies. What had begun as an interesting occurrence of the summer—*Wow! So this is what it's like to live in the eighteen hundreds!*—had quickly turned into a major pain in the butt for everyone.

"Is he coming over?" I whispered.

"No, someone grabbed him. Juliette Bombre. Do you know her?"

With a name like that I had to look. Luc was standing across the street, one hand on his hip but his head was down and an inscrutable look on his face as he listened intently.

Juliette Bombre, who I instantly recognized as the woman who used to sell flowers at the market but had now started selling nuts, was speaking very animatedly to him. She was beautiful in that very French way, meaning effortless and perfect all at once.

I'm not sure why I took an instant dislike to her.

"Jules?"

I turned to Katrine. "What?"

"Another drink?"

I sighed. These informal French lessons with Katrine were getting expensive. I was either going to become fluent at the end of them or an alcoholic. Probably a little of both.

"Sure," I said, not at all sure how I would pay for it.

That seemed to be a recurring theme these days.

❈ ❈ ❈ ❈ ❈

Katrine and I had spent the rest of the afternoon gossiping about the rest of the village or anybody who was hapless enough to walk by our table.

Afterward, I slipped off my shoes and walked barefooted back up the road to my apartment. After three drinks and no lunch, this was one of my brighter decisions.

The slick and very cold marble steps on the winding staircase were worn and slippery and, not for the first time, I wondered how the old ladies made it up and down without killing themselves.

Probably aren't usually snockered for one thing.

"Jules, *es t'il tu?*" one of the old dears sang out from the direction of her apartment.

Madame C and Madame B were twins. One of them had married a few centuries earlier and I had yet to sort out which one that was. In any case they were both single now, in their early nineties, and both veterans of the French Resistance during the last world war.

They had some very interesting stories that they weren't usually in the mood to tell. Even so, over the weeks of shared meals in my apartment over flickering candlelight a few hints had come out and I knew there was something—something *big*—that had happened in the war that they didn't talk about.

Whatever it was I was sure it had to do with the singular sadness that I saw in them from time to time, especially in Madame Cazaly.

"Yep, *c'est moi*," I called up. What with the sudden elimination of a few of our neighbors in the last few weeks, the Madame Twins and I were the only ones left on this side of the apartment building. I know they felt safer with me next door.

Like I'd be able to do squat if we were attacked.

In fact, the two sisters—or *les soeurs* as they were generally known—were a lot better equipped to kick zombie butt than I was should the need arise.

"Did you learn good?" the other sister, Madame Becque, I think, chimed in right about the time I realized these two were learning English a whole lot faster than I was learning French. Maybe we'd meet somewhere in the middle.

"Me very much good," I said in French which made them burst out laughing.

Or maybe not.

As I pushed my apartment door open, both old ladies toddled down the hall toward me. Madame C had a bag of something in her hands. I have no idea where they got half the food they came up with but I'd definitely have starved to death without them by now.

Amazingly, Katrine told me that the two old biddies told *her* the same thing about *me*. Weird.

Right now I was officially subsisting on handouts. Sometimes a bag of food would mysteriously appear on my doorstep—which was probably Luc's doing. When he used to come over more regularly a few weeks back he always brought food. The Madame Twins got a kind of care package from the village because of their age and there was not a moment I didn't feel guilty sharing it with them.

But what else was I going to do?

I have no money over here, an apartment that isn't really mine since I'd swapped my own condo in Atlanta for it and no prospects for being able to support myself.

Usually I tried not to think about where this was all leading.

I'm from the South and trust me when I say the Scarlett O'Hara approach to life is alive and well. I find it works well most of the time. Case in point: I haven't starved yet.

As the old ladies made themselves comfortable in my apartment, I dropped my shoes on the floor and settled onto the couch with my feet on the coffee table. Instantly, the cat Neige jumped up out of nowhere and curled up next to my hip.

He was a strange little cat and not terribly friendly. He definitely considered this apartment his home. I'm not sure what he made of me—the person who more often than not found something for him to eat. But I can say with real satisfaction that he did largely tolerate my presence.

The Poupards—his real owners—were living in my Buckhead condo in Atlanta with my own cat Hamish. I had no idea how they were faring there. Most of the time I thought that I got the raw end of the stick with the whole EMP going off and throwing us functionally back to the 1950's but sometimes at night when I can't sleep I have a nagging suspicion that I am way better off than they are.

"Jules, *la porte!*" Madame C shouted, making me jump. I knew *la porte* meant door but I couldn't for the life of me see how she knew there was someone at the door when as far as I knew nobody had knocked. But sure enough, when I went to the door, I had a visitor.

Thibault Theroux is an acquired taste, I'll say that right off the bat. I've known him five weeks now and he's always been a perfect gentleman and very sweet and yet I still flinch when I first see him. Unctuous, gangly, unkempt, with food usually parked in some part of his straggling beard, he is physically the opposite of his personality which is neat, succinct, good-humored and generous.

We air kissed and I invited him in.

"*Non*, Jules," he said, "I am only coming to tell you a little information and to see if you want to deliver a message to anyone in Aix tomorrow? I am going in the morning."

Thibault had one of the few working vehicles in Chabanel—probably in all of Provence—and the only working ham radio. Aside from those two miracles, he was also very clever with his hands and could put together a contraption to siphon impurities out of your drinking water using bobby pins and old chewing gum.

"I don't know anyone in Aix," I said. The other American in the village, Jim Anderson, had urged me to join the expat community there but so far I hadn't seen the point. "But what's your news?"

I pulled him into the living room and sat him down. Franco social norms dictated that I give him a drink, and ask after his health and his family before getting down to business. What I really wanted to do was grab him by the throat and shriek, *tell me what you know!*

Madame B—knowing the proper etiquette of such things as of course she would—set down a glass of wine in front of him. A raised eyebrow in my direction told me in that universal language of all disproving mothers that she believed I had had quite enough wine myself.

"I have talked to someone in Atlanta," Thibault said.

My stomach muscles tightened. "How bad is it?"

He took a sip of his wine and it was all I could do to sit still.

"Is bad," he said finally. "The outer neighborhoods..."

"The suburbs?"

"*Oui*, the suburbs have created factions."

"They've organized?"

He nodded.

"Is there law enforcement?"

He shook his head. "Not right now."

"I see." I tried to imagine how terrified the Poupards must be in my condo in Buckhead. How were they managing? What were they doing for food?

They're French. Dear God. Do they not have wine?

"But it is not all terrible, I think."

"Really?" I must have looked pathetically hopeful because he patted my hand like I was an old lady asking about specials on laxatives.

"My contact said there is a black market for the necessities."

"Like here."

Thibault waggled his hand as if to say *not quite*.

I think I knew what he meant. In Chabanel, the blackmarket necessities were truffles, *foie gras* and any wine that wasn't made in Provence.

Hey, even in the apocalypse we get tired of drinking rosé all the time!

In Atlanta it was probably more like insulin or clean drinking water. I tried to remember exactly how polluted the Chattahoochee or Lake Lanier were.

"I am sorry, Jules," Thibault said as he finished off his wine and stood up.

I sat for a moment, my thoughts in a swirl. I wondered about my best friend CeCe. *Was she okay? Was she alone?*

Madame C came out of the kitchen with a tray of food in her hands and spoke quickly to Thibault. I assumed she was inviting him to dinner. He gave his apologies before turning toward the door.

"Thibault?" I said impulsively before he left.

"*Si?*"

"May I go with you to Aix tomorrow?"

He grinned. "*Bien sûr.* I will be back at nine tomorrow morning."

When he left, I took my seat at the small dining room table and waited as the old ladies took their places. It was a kind of pasta that looked like hats but had the most divine garlic and tomato sauce and had quickly become one of my most favorite things that the sisters made.

The sisters were devout Catholics and solemnly said grace and crossed themselves before smiling at me.

"Is good, Jules?" Madame Becque said.

"*Oui*, Madame Becque," I said with a sad smile. "Everything considered."

❀ ❀ ❀ ❀ ❀

I wasn't anywhere near consciousness when the pounding on my door roused me that night. There must be something in the walls or in the air or maybe it was the stories that Madame B had been telling last night because I got a vivid image of a Gestapo agent standing on the other side of my door, doing all the pounding.

My basic rule about any kind of knocking on any kind of door that I'm on the other side of in the middle of the night is always *oh hell no.* There was no question of my opening the door.

If it were Luc, he'd say so. Same with anybody else I knew in Chabanel. No, whoever was knocking at my door at three in the morning was not a friend. I stared at the door and held my breath, waiting for the giant axe to come crashing into it or maybe just the sudden emergence of big-ass storm trooper boot as the door erupted into splinters.

A note was shoved underneath.

I didn't touch it at first. When several seconds had passed with no more pounding, I put my ear to the door and listened. It was totally quiet in the hallway. Either whoever was out there had walked away or they were able to wait without breathing. I picked up the note and my hand shook.

The last note I'd had shoved under my door had threatened me with my life.

This time not nearly so bad.

Quickly scanning the note, written in bad English, it seemed that cousins of Sabine and Jacques Poupard were claiming that my apartment was now legally theirs.

I was officially evicted.

2

Where Everybody Knows Your Name

Aix rocks.

I'll tell you that right now.

Having never been to France before and only seeing the south of France in news clips during the Cannes Film Festival, I have to say I didn't really know what to expect.

The trip to Aix with Thibault gave me no clue as to the wonders that would await. First, it was a fairly drab drive—all warehouses and brown grass with a few more nondescript exits leading to more nondescript villages.

Thibault chattered on about some deal he was doing in Aix with some other gizmo gadget kind of guy but unless it involved making the lights go back on this afternoon I wasn't really interested.

I'd had some time to put together my thoughts about my three o'clock mail delivery and I still wasn't sure it wasn't some kind of joke. Although granted it was not at all funny I've learned during my time here that most jokes in France are not at all funny. In any case, whether it was a gag or these people really were intent on taking my apartment, I made sure the place was securely locked before I left this morning. If these "cousins" were the real deal, I'd work something out with them later. Tomorrow. Or next month.

I *have* mentioned my Scarlett O'Hara tendencies, haven't I?

Anyway as I said, I wasn't at all sure what to expect in Aix. The streets were vacant for the most part. Some people had set up booths and kiosks in an impromptu market on the ring road around Aix and there were several cars and trucks stranded at various spots on the D7N which Thibault had to maneuver around, but for the most part it was as I'd expected.

Until we got to the town itself and then...wow.

It was so much bigger and lusher and more...everything than little Chabanel. There were massive plane trees lining both sides of the main avenue that dappled the whole street with golden light.

I could totally see why famous artists would want to live and die here.

Thibault had to be mindful of where he parked his car—as in he really couldn't. Owning a working vehicle in post-apocalyptic France was like owning a flying carpet or the last bottle of vodka in Russia. Thibault was a big guy and unless he was rushed by a mob—not unimaginable in Tampa or Charlotte but not likely in Provence—nobody was wrestling the car keys away from him. Even so he certainly couldn't leave *me* to watch the car while he ran errands on foot.

As I jotted down all the places and things he wanted me to do while he circled the city it did occur to me that perhaps Thibault had had this in mind all along. After all, if I hadn't asked to come, how in the world would he have done it alone?

Stowing my less than generous thoughts, I took Thibault's shopping list and the mail pouch he had stuffed full of correspondence and got out of the car. Since he would have to more or less keep on the move we made plans to meet in front of the Apple store at three o'clock or as the French perversely insist on referring to it, fifteen hundred hours.

The Apple store was right at the beginning of this gorgeous main pedestrian drag called the Cours Mirabeau which was punctuated with ancient and weird fountains. One looked like a giant fur ball with no discernable spouting water that I could detect.

Since I didn't see the Apple store when it was actually selling laptops and cellphones, I can't tell you how amazing it must have been before the EMP but it was still extremely cool now. It was a huge building that was glass on all sides and not a single crack in any of it. It stood as testimony to how civilized the French truly are.

Can you imagine an all glass monument to consumer elitism surviving one night of the apocalypse in Atlanta, Georgia? Seriously?

Anyway, the store was now filled with long tables loaded w ith nonedible goods in a sort of indoor market protected from the elements.

Thibault let me out and I have to say there were so many people strolling along with their dogs, or lovers walking hand in hand, smiling and relaxing, that it was difficult to imagine that the EMP had hit here too. The ambience was relaxed and congenial.

The outdoor cafés that lined the Cours Mirabeau were full of people drinking coffee and eating pastries. Obviously the mayor of Aix had given its population the same inspiring nationalistic speech that the Chabanel mayor had delivered to us.

Everyone appeared to be working very hard to behave like it was business-as-usual which, in France, means enjoying life to the fullest.

And the people in Aix obviously knew exactly how to do that.

Once I'd walked the length of the Cours Mirabeau I resolved to come back and sit at one of these cafés before I had to meet Thibault. One of the cafés boasted it had been open since 1792! Certainly one dirty bomb over the Mediterranean wasn't going to stop *it* from serving its patrons *foie gras* and beer!

Thibault had several things on the list he'd given me. Many tasks just involved delivering notes and letters to various addresses but the bulk of the "mail" went to one address which it turned out was an ad hock post office housed in what used to be the natural history museum.

I'm not sure if the so-called post office was government run, sanctioned or just a pal of Thibault's, but the guy—chain-smoking and ogling me as he took my packet of mail seemed to know right what to do with it.

After that I had several places I delivered small packets of things to. The packets felt clunky and mechanical and I assumed they were gadgets Thibault created that somehow made life after the EMP more bearable for people. I should ask him if I could have one. Whatever they were.

The drill was simple. I would knock on a door, hand the person who answered a piece of paper with a message from Thibault. They would then hand me money and I'd fork over the little parcel. I did this about five times.

Since I wasn't sure what kind of law enforcement was in force in Aix, I was a tad nervous about jingling around the back streets of a major town with a slowly growing amount of coins and bills in my bag, but honestly I was so distracted by how beautiful Aix was —and how unaffected it was by the EMP—that I soon forgot to be nervous.

Why hadn't I done a house swap in Aix? Here they have their choice among hundreds of bakeries and bars, not just two.

Just as I was about to reward myself for my morning with a lovely sit-down at one of the cafés along the Cours Mirabeau, I saw something that quite literally stopped me in my tracks.

It was a store front unlike the other stores on this street. I'd passed many elegant shops and boutiques—some even still open for business—but this shop looked like the quintessential high end jewelry store complete with spot lighting picking out the golden essence of its products which were beautifully arranged on three tiers of glass shelving in the display window.

Toile netting and silk bows were in every color of the color wheel and artfully arranged on each shelf to better enhance the presentation of the store's treasures.

It was amazing to realize that this store must have used a professional display artist to arrange its window. There could be no other explanation for its pleasingly artful presentation.

Did I mention it was a pastry shop?

And not just any pastry shop, I thought, figuratively wiping the drool from the corner of my mouth as I approached, stunned and delighted by its presentation of glory, but one that also sold chocolates, each obviously hand crafted and decorated like a work of art.

I tore my eyes away from the amazing store window to see the name of the shop in tall gold letters over the glass door.

Ducharme. Pâtissier et Confiseur d'Aix.

Not surprisingly, the queue of customers snaked out the door. Without another moment's hesitation, I took my place in line.

❈ ❈ ❈ ❈ ❈

Luc stood in the mayor's office and tried very hard to keep his cool.

Mayor Beaufait had done everything in her power to create an ambience inside her office that appeared unaffected by last month's EMP. In Luc's mind it was counterproductive on every level to allow the villagers to see that *their* reality was not also the mayor's.

But as Lola had pointed out on more than one occasion, she had been in office for more than twenty years so whatever she did and however she did it was obviously fine with the people of Chabanel.

"What about the water supply?" Mayor Beaufait was asking him now. She sat at her desk and steepled her long manicured fingernails as if in serious reflection.

"We have an untainted reservoir that will serve us well enough," Luc said with all the patience he could manage. It was not his job to keep the mayor informed of the waterline on the village cistern. She knew this as well as he. The random comment was a message to him that she had no quarrel with how he was running the village *police municipale*.

She only had a problem that may or may not be within her jurisdiction to harangue him about.

Jules Hooker.

In the last few weeks Luc had done everything in his power to push Jules out of his mind and out of his life. Not that he wasn't imminently fascinated and charmed by the outspoken American. *Au contraire*. It was *because* he was so enamored of her that he knew he needed to create some distance between them.

Especially since, as far as the mayor was concerned, Jules would always be a sticking point. Ever

22

since it became clear that the Americans had prompted Iran's retaliation with a nuclear bomb that exploded over the Mediterranean, Beaufait and other nationalistic politicians had not made secret their desire to sever connections with the US.

Not that that mattered.

At least not unless you were an American stranded in Provence with no money, no place to live and no friends.

"I am informed that you are continuing to aid and support the American on rue Gaston de Saporta?" Beaufait said as if reading his mind.

"Your information is incorrect," Luc said between gritted teeth. "The Cazaly sisters receive a food box— as does every veteran and citizen over the age of sixty as per your instructions."

"She lives with them, does she not?"

"If by *she*, you refer to the American, she does not, no. She lives in the same building."

"I thought I told you to send her to Aix."

"Banishment without a crime is not within my power," Luc said tightly.

"Are you being flippant with me?"

"The American Consulate in Aix is closed," Luc said. "What would you have me do? Dump her in the middle of the Cours Mirabeau?"

Beaufait narrowed her eyes and Luc cursed the second sense that most French women seemed to have when it came to Frenchmen.

We may be mysteries to every other woman on earth, but to a Frenchwoman, we will always be naked and open.

Before she could openly accuse him of unfairly obliging or favoring Jules, Luc said briskly, "I am not able to expel US Nationals—or anyone for that matter —without due cause."

"Very well, Luc," the mayor said, with a shrug as if bored with the conversation. "That is all."

As Luc turned to leave, Beaufait cleared her throat and he stopped without turning around.

"I will, of course, be happy to give you due cause, Chief DeBray," the mayor said. "should that become necessary."

3

The Days Grow Colder

Believe it or not the three people scurrying around the inside of *Ducharme* with little gold tongs placing amazing puff pastry creations in crisp white bags were all wearing white shirts and little black ties like they were a team of synchronized waiters at a fancy restaurant.

The closer I got to the front counter the more impossible I realized it was going to be to select something.

The glass display counter had another three shelves full of pastries in such abundance it was hard to believe so many would be eaten before the end of the day.

There was row upon row of glossy bright red berry tarts and glistening logs of chocolate éclairs, fat flaky croissants, and perfect stacks of sugar cookies with chunks of crystallized sugar dusting the tops as big as tacks.

Dear God how do the French eat like this and fit through normal-sized doorways?

When I got to the front I saw that two of the scurrying tong-wielders were attractive if unsmiling young women. An older woman stood by the no-longer functioning cash register.

Her face was pinched and tense as she watched the crowd and I couldn't help think she was the antithesis of the delightful promise made by the front display window.

Just as I was about to say to myself that the owners really should jettison this sourpuss for the negative PR she was projecting, one of the women behind me called out to her by name: *Madame Ducharme*.

Wow. She owns all this sugar and still looks like she's sucking a lemon?

Madame Ducharme nodded at the person in recognition and then turned sharply aside to address someone behind her. It was then that I saw there was a half-open curtain behind her that led to a hidden room.

Must be where the magic happens, I thought with anticipation. I intended to get six cream puffs and a dozen chocolate éclairs. Apocalypse be damned.

Just as I came to the counter and began rehearsing the words, "*Me want that and that and this many of that*," while pointing like a five-year-old, I noticed that the gap in the curtain widened and a man's face appeared.

A very ugly, very angry man's face.

In a flash, he reached out and grabbed Madame Ducharme by the nose and pulled her into the back room.

I was so astonished I wasn't sure I'd really seen it. I stood at the counter, my mouth open, when one of the officious young women addressed me and snapped out, "*Que désirez-vous, Madame?*"

I stuttered, forgot which pastries to point at, and was unceremoniously pushed out of my place in line by the people behind me.

❋ ❋ ❋ ❋ ❋

Luc walked around his desk and picked up the stack of notecards that Eloise had dropped there an hour earlier. While he'd found a few moments during the last few weeks to be grateful that the phone wasn't ringing off the hook any more, he recognized that the problem with no phone service meant his waiting room was usually full of people—irate, angry people.

He was about to toss the packet back in his in-basket when his eye caught the name *Cazaly*.

"Eloise!" he barked to his sergeant whose office was in the adjoining room.

Eloise Basile appeared in the doorway, an expectant look on her face. Even when he yelled at her or asked her to fetch him coffee, Eloise—unlike his second-in-command Adrien Matteo—never complained or let an insolent smirk cross her face.

He waved the notecard. "What is the trouble with *les soeurs*?"

"They wouldn't say, Chief. Just that it had to be you and they'd wait for as long as it took."

"Which you took to mean it wasn't urgent?"

Eloise's smile dropped from her face.

"I'm sorry, Chief if I—"

"No, no, that is a part of your job, is it not? To triage and assess?" He softened his tone with a smile. "So neither of them was bleeding?"

She blushed with relief.

"I think they are just lonely with the American out of town," she said.

He nodded and tossed the notecard down. He was sure it was nothing. Just a couple of old ladies unhappy at being left alone after they'd gotten use to Jules' company and attention.

Jules' attention was mildly addicting.

He pulled on his jacket. "I will take an early lunch and swing by and see them."

✿ ✿ ✿ ✿ ✿

I won't say the little *contretemps* between the owner of Ducharme's and the man behind the curtain ruined my experience at the *pâtisserie*. I did manage to get my pastries and once I took them to a nearby park bench and plowed through two of them without taking a breath, I felt much recovered from it all.

Or once my sugar craving was satisfied I was able to think more clearly about what it was I'd seen.

If Madame Ducharme was the owner of the *pâtisserie*—and now that I thought back on it she wasn't wearing fancy clothes like the servers were, she was wearing a white chef's jacket—then who else might presume to treat her like that if not *Monsieur* Ducharme?

Not very pretty for the buying public to have to witness although it was possible I was the only one who saw.

Does this mean the person who creates all that confectionary magic is an abused woman?

I dusted flakes of sugar and pastry from my slacks.

"Jules?"

I looked up to see Jim Anderson striding toward me, a surprised grin on his face.

"What are you doing in Aix?" he said as he leaned over to kiss my cheek.

"I came in with a friend," I said, genuinely delighted to see him.

"I see you've discovered the jewel in Aix's crown." He gestured to my Ducharme's bag. "Listen, some of the other expats are meeting for *apéros* this evening. Why don't you come?"

"I'm supposed to meet my ride," I said hesitantly. Honestly, the idea of hanging with a bunch of people who all spoke English sounded real good to me right now. And Jim's crinkly blue eyes and big expansive manner—so American!—felt real good too.

"Tell your ride you'll come back to Chabanel with me tomorrow morning."

"Really?"

Why did that sound so good? Was a part of me dreading going back to the village to sort out the whole apartment ownership thing? Or was the magic of Aix just so alluring?

"Where would I stay?"

"The Hotel Cezanne is choc-a-block with Americans who got caught when the EMP went off. I'm sure the proprietor can find it in his heart to house one more for a night or two. It's not like too many people are coming to Aix these days on vacation."

Thirty minutes later, I met Thibault, handed over the money and the empty mail pouch and air-kissed him goodbye. I had no idea what he'd gotten up to in his day and I didn't ask.

An hour after that I sat out under the plane trees at the Nina Café with Jim, feeling lighter and more at peace than I had in weeks. I couldn't help but think that *this* is what I'd had in mind all along when I first came to the south of France: a lovely cool champagne cocktail in one hand, a very hunky guy who couldn't take his eyes off me and a bunch of new friends all laughing and talking at once.

Although it seems the expat community in Aix is quite large, there were only a handful actually living in Aix when the bomb dropped. Two Americans from Indianapolis, Jane and Glenn White, were in Aix visiting their son, Elliott, who was a student at the University of Aix.

They had been staying at the Hotel Cezanne which is where they met Joanne and Barry Simpson from Charleston, who were both investment bankers and just as stuck and broke as I was.

The EMP. The Great Leveler.

After we all swapped our *where were you when the lights went out* stories, I settled into the conversational swing of getting to know everyone.

Elliott was there too and at twenty-five I would have said he was a little old to still be living overseas claiming a student visa. He was sullen and ill-humored and I would have said he was a little old for that too.

"Glenn and I were just about to fly back home when the EMP happened," Jane said. "A part of me was so relieved, you know?"

Everyone laughed. "No, Jane," Jim said. "How in the world could you be pleased about such a thing?"

She shrugged and looked at Elliott. She didn't have to explain. Because if she'd gotten on that airplane *after* the EMP she'd possibly never have seen her son again. I definitely got a chill.

"Elliott has done so well in his classes here in Aix," Jane said. "And his French is fluent."

"It helps that he has a French girlfriend," Glenn said, looking at his son approvingly to polite laughter from the rest of us.

"She works at Ducharme's," Jane said. "Have you been?"

"I was just there!" I said. "That place is amazing!" I looked at Elliott but he just looked away.

"But I think Monsieur Ducharme might be a pig," I said to Jane. "I saw Madame Ducharme and as she was standing there in the store some guy reached over and grabbed her by the nose!"

Jane and Joanne both gasped and looked at Jim. "Is that a French thing?" Jane asked.

"How would I know?" he said with a grin. "But I'll check the weekly newsletter they send out about Frenchmen and their typical behavior."

"Well, it's abhorrent," Joanne said as she dabbed at the lipstick on her champagne glass with a tissue.

"Her husband is a bastard," Elliott said and all eyes turned to him in surprise. "Well, he is," he said defensively. "He's always ragging on Agnes."

"Is that your girlfriend? She must have been one of the ones I saw waiting on customers," I said. "What does she look like?"

"Why?" Elliott said, narrowing his eyes.

"Elliott!" Jane said. "Don't be rude." She turned to me and smiled. "She's the pretty one with long dark hair to her waist and big brown eyes."

I remembered her. The other girl was blonde. In fact, now that I thought of it, the other one looked like Madame Ducharme.

"Is the other server a member of the family?" I asked.

"Who are you?" Elliott said with an ugly twist to his mouth. "Sixty Minutes?"

"Elliott, I will not have you—" Glenn began, his face darkening with anger.

"No, it's okay," I said. "Elliott's right. I'm a reporter. Or at least I was. Even my friends tell me I have a tendency to interrogate. Sorry, Elliott."

He shrugged and looked at his nails.

I turned to Joanne and Barry or, as I referred to them in my mind, *the rich ones*.

"I'm thinking of working as a private investigator. So if you know someone who might be interested in my services, I'd appreciate it if you'd pass my name around."

"A private investigator?" Jim said with a frown. "Really? Is there money in that?"

"We'll see," I said cheerfully. In fact, after my third champagne I was feeling quite insanely optimistic about my chances of making a living as a private eye.

Jane laughed. "I heard Monsieur Benet who runs the hotel lost his dog. Perhaps you could help him?"

Everyone laughed, me included.

Jim leaned over to say in a loud stage whisper, "Somebody probably ate it."

The women threw their cocktail napkins at him in mock horror as the men laughed good-naturedly. That's the thing I've noticed about men. Most of them don't like to think handsome men are funny. I'm not sure handsome men are very often funny but most men don't like it and will only laugh begrudgingly.

Hey. I'm trained to notice these things.

"Don't say that," Joanne said with a smile. "This is France. Can you imagine? Detroit, maybe, but Provence? Never."

That was a bit of gallows humor that we could all have done without and in fact I rather lay the blame for the resultant downturn of the evening on that splash of cold water reminding us that we were not here on a jolly holiday but unable to return to our country—a country that was struggling daily to survive.

As the evening wore on, I felt more and more of the magic of my day fade. I'm not sure what it was beyond Joanne's not-so-funny comment. Maybe I was just tired from all the things I'd seen and done that day.

But if I were honest I'd have to say that as I sat back and studied these very nice people who were speaking my language and laughing and making me feel so much at home, that I couldn't help thinking about the Madame Twins and wondering how they were doing.

And Luc. I was thinking of Luc, too, although I wasn't really wondering how *he* was doing. Luc DeBray was a very capable man and I had every confidence that he was doing just fine.

But perhaps that was the champagne talking.

❀ ❀ ❀ ❀ ❀

My watch said it was not yet five in the morning when the pounding began. At first unsure whether the pounding was all in my head—and I'd certainly had enough *Kir Royales* last night to warrant it—or only on the outside of my hotel room door, I lay in bed and let the two merge together in a cacophony of noise.

"Jules! Please, open up!"

American words, I thought groggily as I swung my legs out of bed. I'd slept in my silk singlet and bikini briefs but my naked toes touched carpet that had to be an inch thick. I grabbed my jacket and staggered toward the door.

I opened it to see the distraught face of Jane White.

I glanced down the hall but didn't smell smoke.

"Jules, you have to help me," Jane said as she stood in the hallway of the Cezanne Hotel wringing her hands.

What kind of help could she possible need at five in the morning with the hotel clearly not on fire?

I opened the door wider to let her in. But she didn't come in. Instead, she took a step backward as if she wanted me to follow her.

"Hurry, Jules! It's Elliott. The police have taken him."

That made me wake up in a hurry. I pulled my jacket around me, all of a sudden very aware of noises coming up the spiral staircase from the hotel lobby, and of my bare thighs showing beneath my short jacket.

"Elliott? Why?" I asked.

Now I could definitely hear the sounds of men's voices in the lobby. Officious mens' voices. Loud, hard men's voices.

"What's happened?" I asked in bewilderment.

"They think he killed her!" Jane said, following my eyes toward the spiral staircase where the voices were coming.

"Who?"

"Madame Ducharme! She was murdered last night!"

5

Chateau of Cards

It took me all of five minutes to put on yesterday's clothes and run downstairs with Jane right behind me. I had no idea what she thought I could do but when I got to the lobby I saw that Jim was in the middle of the room, running a hand through his thick hair, and speaking with two exceedingly greasy looking Mediterranean looking men in sloppy jackets and pointy shoes. Their faces and their clothes screamed *police detectives*.

Monsieur Benet, the proprietor of the Hotel Cezanne, stood behind the registration counter as if he expected to start checking people in, except his face looked horror-struck and his hands were bunched into fists on the hotel ledger. His eyes went back and forth from Jim to the detectives.

Jane went immediately to her husband Glenn who was standing beside Jim, his face grim and ashen.

Several other guests were huddled in the lobby. I don't know why but I could just tell they didn't speak French because they looked as befuddled as I was.

The minute I reached Jim, the two detectives turned and left the hotel. As soon as they did it was like air exploding out of a balloon. All the people in the lobby clustered around Jim.

"What did they say?"

"Why did they take Elliott?"

"Did he really kill the woman?"

"Is the bakery going to be closed? I was just on my way there!"

Jim took my hand and nodded to Jane and Glenn to follow him into the office behind the counter. I saw Joanne watching us with wide eyes but she didn't follow. I didn't see Barry with her.

As soon as Jim closed the door behind him, Jane collapsed into her husband's arms, her shoulders shaking with her sobs. Glenn's face was solemn and pinched as he faced Jim.

"Well?" Glenn said.

Jim ran his hand through his hair again and I recognized it as a gesture he made when he was frustrated or confounded or both.

"Nicole Ducharme found her mother Marine Ducharme about six hours ago," Jim said. "She was dead in her bakery."

"But why did they take Elliott?" Jane wailed, her face mottled with tears.

Jim sighed. "They said they found a note in the kitchen signed by Elliott threatening Madame Ducharme."

"I don't believe it!" Jane gasped. "It's a lie."

Jim turned to her, sadly. "They say they have it, Jane. And there are ways to prove its authenticity. Even now."

"But the note is merely circumstantial," Glenn said. "For whatever idiot reason the boy wrote it, it doesn't mean he killed her."

"I know," Jim said. "Except he wasn't home last night and it seems nobody can vouch for where he was."

"I can!" Jane said. "He was with me. Wasn't he, Glenn?"

But Glenn only shook his head and looked out the window of the office as if he'd heard enough.

"There's more," Jim said. "They have an eyewitness."

"To the *murder*?" Glenn sputtered in surprise.

"No, but someone out walking his dog saw a man who fits Elliott's description coming out of the bakery at the time of the murder."

"That's a lie!" Janie said again, this time looking at me as if for corroboration. I could only imagine what she must be feeling.

"The detective said Elliott admitted he was at the bakery last night," Jim said.

"I don't believe this," Glenn said, shaking his head again. "I don't believe any of this."

Jane turned to me and grabbed my hand.

"You have to help us, Jules," she said plaintively.

"Me?" I squeaked.

"Yes. You said you do investigative work. You have to help us prove Elliott's innocence. Please!"

I have to say even though I'd been thinking of doing something like this for weeks I'd never moved it out of the fantasy stage into the reality stage so I just stood there with my mouth open.

"I...I'm not sure I..."

I looked at Jim who was frowning and in that instant I realized he didn't want me to do this. He didn't want me to get their hopes up or to interfere with an official police investigation. He didn't want me to get involved.

I turned back to Jane.

"Of course, I'll help," I said, squeezing her hand.

❀❀❀❀❀

After learning from Jane that Elliott had been intending to spend the night with his girlfriend Agnes—and after successfully avoiding any more disapproving glances from Jim—I ran back upstairs to my room to freshen up and try to make my clothes look as if I hadn't slept in them.

It was nearer to nine in the morning when I came back downstairs. Monsieur Benet gave me a nod as I did. He and I had already half-joked about my finding his missing dog for him in exchange for a room at the hotel. I was pretty sure he knew that young men being held on false murder charges trumped runaway dogs.

While delighted to have my first official case I have to say a couple things bothered me as I hurried down the street toward the Cours Mirabeau.

First, I'd just made a promise to a very distraught woman that I would help free her son when I did not speak French so I wasn't exactly sure how I was going to question any of the people involved to get the necessary answers to free Elliott.

And secondly, I did not know if Elliott was really innocent.

Details, details, I chided myself as I reached Aix's grand boulevard. The Ducharme bakery was on rue Thiers just off the Cours Mirabeau but I was headed toward the student section of town which was where I was hoping to find Agnes Valentin.

If she really *was* with Elliott last night, this would be the fastest paycheck I ever earned.

I slowed my pace. Would the Whites pay me *less* if I did this quickly? I wondered. Would they pay me more? I shook the irrelevant thoughts from my head. *Just do the job as quickly and the best you can. That's all.*

But I couldn't help think that if Agnes were to confirm Elliott's alibi, I'd have the rest of the afternoon to shop at some of the amazing boutiques I was passing —charmingly avant-garde boutiques with names like *Promod* and *Cosmoparis* and *Bada*—and I'd do it with money in my pocket for a change.

My exploration yesterday through this section of Aix on behalf of Thibault and his mildly dubious dealings had given me a vague familiarity with the area. I had Agnes's student apartment address and I knew some of the university was on the other side of the main market district on the Place Richelmé.

As I walked I noted the roads were largely pedestrian-only which hardly mattered since there were no longer any working vehicles. I was passed by a few ancient scooters but when the petrol rations ran out they would be parked somewhere or stripped for parts until the world righted itself—if it ever did.

The roads were hardly as wide as an alley and they all had shallow rain gutters running down the middle instead of on the sides as we did in the US. The gutters ran in each direction to sewer openings framed by raised cobblestones.

Like in Chabanel, the buildings in Aix were mostly made of limestone in a wide range of hues from lemon yellow to golden ochre. Sunlight on the buildings made them seem to glow.

No wonder people love the south of France, I thought inanely as I hurried down the bumpy alley, nodding to shoppers and strollers as I went. The sun was already hot at mid morning.

I couldn't help but notice that a lot of people were walking their dogs and I was surprised that more hadn't been made of that in all the travel brochures I'd ever seen.

I was also surprised to see so many feral cats—they were literally everywhere—and that too was strangely absent from the plethora of travel advertising.

I watched a blonde poodle walk primly next to its owner without even a leash to control it or make it mind, and I thought of the mysterious witness who said he'd seen Elliott. Supposedly he had been out at midnight walking his dog. Somehow I needed to get his identity from the cops.

On both sides of the streets were Aix's trademark golden yellow buildings with blue shutters and stark black wrought iron Juliette balconies and grills on the bottom windows.

Although some of the shops were closed and boards had been nailed across all the ATM machines, a surprising number of shops including *L'Occitane de Provence* and even Monoprix—the large French department store—were still open for business.

As was every single bakery or *pâtisserie* that I passed.

Not even the apocalypse can get between the French and their croissants.

As I reached the Place Richelmé, I saw that the market was in the process of being dismantled in order that the café tables could be put in their place. The cobblestones were wet where the merchants had hosed down the stones in front of the fishmonger's booth or where the fishmonger had dumped his ice. It made me wonder where in the world they were getting ice?

That's the true mystery of the apocalypse, I thought. Not who bombed us or how can we survive now, but how do the fish sellers keep their cod cold?

Focused on getting past the slippery stones of the disintegrating market without ending up sprawled eagle on them, I jumped when I heard a horn honk not fifteen feet from me.

Because I wasn't expecting to see a car, it took me a moment to recognize Thibault's 2CV idling in the rue Mejanes. I squinted and a large beefy arm shot out of the window to wave at me.

"Thibault!" I called, feeling irrationally happy to come across someone familiar. Carefully picking my way across the slick cobblestones I made my way over to him and we air kissed our greeting.

"I am so glad to see you, Jules," he said. "Are you coming home?"

"You're not going to believe this," I said with excitement. "I've been hired to find a murderer!"

"*C'est vrai?*" he said, his eyes round with surprise.

"Well, technically I've been hired to prove a man's innocence," I amended. "But the easiest way to do that is to find out who really killed the victim."

Thibault nodded and I have to say I'd have expected a little more enthusiasm from him at my announcement. I soon found out why he was less than impressed with my new job.

"*Les soeurs* are missing you," he said. "Do you have a message for them?"

"Tell them I'll be back soon and I'll bring lots of gifts when I do. Are they eating okay, do you know?"

He nodded. "*Bien sûr*. Chabanel is looking out for them." He hesitated and licked his lips.

"What?" I said. "Is there more?"

"Perhaps," he said hesitantly. "Perhaps a little problem."

"Problem? What problem?" I felt a tightening in my chest.

"It is just..." His eyes glanced around the market as if intently interested in how the workers were tearing down the stands.

"Thibault, please spit it out," I said impatiently. "Has something happened?"

"I am to tell you that your things are safe," he said reluctantly.

I felt my heart begin to beat faster.

"What does that mean? Stop being so cryptic. Why wouldn't my things be safe?"

"The new people are living in your apartment now. I am being so sorry, Jules! But your clothes, they are with *les soeurs*." He spoke quickly as if to get it all out in a rush and have it over with.

I gaped at him for a moment.

"They broke into my apartment?!"

"I think they had a key."

"They can't do this! I'll go to the police!"

Thibault winced.   "Jules, *mais non*. It was the police who took your things out."

"I don't believe it! I'll tell Luc! He'll...he'll—"

 Thibault shook his head sadly.

"Chief DeBray was the one who did it," he said.

5

The Slow Burn

I was so shocked I barely remember saying goodbye to Thibault.

My stuff thrown in the street? By Luc DeBray?

I stood on the corner of the quickly disappearing market, my mouth open in frank astonishment.

Am I homeless?

"*Pardon, Madame*," a man said after rudely bumping into me but effectively waking me up to my surroundings. I rubbed the elbow he'd whacked with his briefcase and forced myself to recalibrate and pull myself together.

Well, good, I thought. *That settles that. I like Aix better than Chabanel anyway. I'll just go collect my clothes, say goodbye to the Madame Twins, and see what I have to do to get a permanent room at the Hotel Cezanne.*

In fact, this is perfect.

I glanced at the slip of paper in my hand where Jane had jotted down Agnes Valentin's address and turned from the noisy hubbub of the market-turned-café square.

As soon as I turned onto the nearest road adjacent to the market, I saw that it opened into yet another square—this one full of people selling flowers. Or at least had been a few hours earlier.

Now the cobblestones were littered with torn leaves and straw in a half inch of water. Somehow Aix had access to water hoses with water.

See? Everything about Aix is better.

I walked in front of a government building with three sets of French flags hanging over the double doors and noted that this must be their *place de Maire*—site of the city hall. In many ways it was just a larger version of Chabanel's. It was ringed by a narrow road, now clear of any vehicles, with a line of storefronts and cafés beyond that.

A giant clock tower was set in an ancient nearby archway. As I passed through the archway, I saw a plaque that I'm sure told the interesting history of the clock tower or the square or both. But I was in a hurry and besides I couldn't understand the words anyway.

Continuing down the street, I came to *la place des Martyrs de Résistance*. This was a big cobblestone square lined on three sides by six plane trees. A chill ran through me as I imagined young people with Nazi nooses around their necks standing where there was now a pizzeria.

I kept moving.

Past the martyrs square was a huge church that I thought must be the local cathedral. The double wooden doors were so massive they were taller than the first floor of my condo building back in Atlanta. Mildly curious, I scanned the front of the church for any sign of a name but found none.

Directly across from the church was a dark yellow limestone building with window boxes full of red geraniums in each of the windows on the first three floors.

I straightened my blouse the best I could so that it might not look as if I'd slept in it. I was fully aware of the reputation most French women had about their clothes and their appearance in general. I had no desire to appear the typical unkempt or clueless American. My favorite Jimmy Choo sandals were badly scuffed but there was nothing I could do about that. I walked up to the single colossal carved wooden door and rang the bell.

I expected to have to fumble through a painful exchange in Franglish but luckily it seems students are irreverent the world over. I was buzzed in without a word.

Inside was a courtyard leading to another door which revealed a lobby with yet another spiral staircase. I quickly checked the mailbox and found *A. Valentin Chambre* 6. I went to the first floor, saw there were only three apartments on the floor, and went up to the next floor where I quickly found Apartment 6 and knocked on the door.

While I assumed the cops had already questioned Agnes—since she was the girlfriend of their prime suspect and also because she worked at the Ducharme's —I was less confident that they did so in order to confirm Elliott's alibi. Call me cynical, but they had their guy. Finding reasons why they *didn't* have their guy would not be something they'd put much effort into.

I didn't have to wait long. The door opened and the girl who'd waited on me and hundreds of others yesterday at Ducharme's stood in the doorway glaring at me. She rattled off something harsh to me in French.

"Sorry," I said smiling brightly. "Do you speak English?"

I knew she did. First, she was a student and secondly, her boyfriend was American.

"Who are you?" she asked.

I know Jane had said she was pretty and yesterday, with the flattering lights in the bakery and all the excitement and anticipation of sugar imploding, I'd thought the same. But either Agnes had been up all night on a bender or she was criminally plain. Either way I wanted to say, *Smile, honey! It makes even homely girls less homely!*

"I'm a friend of Elliott White's," I said. "Do you have a minute to talk?"

"I have already talked with the police. I know nothing."

Did she even know her boyfriend was in jail?

"I was hoping you might help me help Elliott," I said. "The police think he was the one who...hurt Madame Ducharme."

The girl let out an impatient snort. I guess that answered the question of whether or not she knew about Elliott's arrest. Clearly she knew and didn't give a crap.

"He said he was with you last night," I said.

I think right about now was when I knew she was going to say she hadn't been with him. It was only a few seconds after that I started thinking maybe I'd been a little hasty on the whole *I'll take this case and prove your son innocent* thing.

"He wasn't with me last night," she said, gripping the door and obviously just about to slam it in my face. "I told the police that and now I'll tell you. We only went out twice. I told him last week I didn't want to see him again. Are we done?"

I usually pride myself on having a clever come back and unlike some people, it doesn't take me long to put one together. I'm not often the one walking away imagining what I *could* have said.

But this time I was still standing there with my mouth open and the sound of the door slamming shut ringing in my ears.

6

A Few Buns Short

I walked back toward my hotel as if in a fog. What Agnes had told me was *not* good for Elliott. It wasn't good for me either if it turned out I was trying to prove a guilty man was innocent.

The first question I had as I walked away was why had Elliott been talking to Madame Ducharme in the first place? Why did he write the threatening note to her? What exactly did that threatening note say?

And if Elliott and Agnes were no longer together, why did he visit her boss?

None of it made much sense but as I walked the narrow winding stone streets of Aix heading toward its grand avenue, I forced myself to think about it because otherwise I'd end up thinking about Luc's betrayal.

Betrayal. That's a good word. It's practically onomatopoeic. It *sounds* like what it is. *Betrayal.* I forced thoughts of Luc away.

As I walked, I looked idly at the shop fronts and even though this section of Aix was by no means upscale, the shops were still elegant and expensive. Plus there had to be at least one children's clothing store for every three other stores.

What is with the French and their kids?

While I saw most French women wearing largely black for their look—*très dated* if you ask me—their children were all mix and matched in the most precious colors and outfits. Even the boys! Maybe French women decided they'd rather get fat after all and gave up the fashion crown in favor of dressing up their kids?

As I got closer to the Cours Mirabeau I noticed that the cobblestone avenues became wider and more and more shops featured large stone planters with lush plantings. It was almost park-like with the overall effect one of tranquility and luxury.

Did I mention that Aix is a city of fountains? But while most of the ones I saw weren't working—as in *none* of them—I couldn't say whether that was because of the EMP or it had always been that way.

But if it had, I'd be surprised. Even when times are desperate, the French strike me as a people who like pretty things. Maybe *especially* when times are desperate.

Sure enough, the natty little street that I was on soon emptied out onto the Cours Mirabeau where the vibe was instantly energetic. I'd seen a few café tables wedged into the narrow alleys but now they were spilling out onto the sidewalk, edging onto the verge of the famous boulevard. And while it was barely noon, every single table was full.

I decided to enjoy the lovely weather—and possibly put off the walk back to the hotel where I might have to ask Jane and Glenn White if there was any way their son might have killed Marine Ducharme after all since frankly all signs pointed to it.

Yeah, a nice walk in the sunshine first, I thought.

I hadn't gone twenty steps before I noticed that I was nearing the by-way where Ducharme's *pâtisserie* was located. Expecting to see fluttering reels of yellow crime scene tape, I was astonished to see that while the bakery was closed there was no other indication that something violent had happened here recently.

I walked to the front of the store. A blind had been pulled over the front display window. Either there was nothing to see on the display shelves—which would damage the magic of the Ducharme brand—or there *was* something to see and it was all stale and falling apart.

Same diff really.

Even so, I swear I could detect the scent of baking confections surrounding the bakery. I stood for a moment and watched the front, remembering how yesterday the front door had been crammed with customers, the line out the front and down the street.

All those people. Had they gone to other bakeries?

Ducharme's tragedy would be another pastry shop's good fortune.

Suddenly I heard a loud muffled clanging and I walked a few steps past the bakery to see around the corner of the building to a tiny alleyway that led to the back of the shop. Two metal garbage cans sat pushed up against an old stone wall in the alley. Standing in the alley was the other serving girl I remembered from yesterday.

Nicole Ducharme.

I hurried down the alley, not sure exactly what I was going to say but realizing this was a break for me.

"*Excusez-moi!*" I said as I reached her. "Hello. Do you speak English?"

She looked startled as if I'd just materialized in front of her.

"I am so sorry about your loss," I said, remembering my manners. "My sympathies to you and your whole family."

"What do you want?"

Good news: she speaks English. Bad news: she's a bitch.

"Well, you see, a friend of mine, Elliott White, has been arrested...in connection, you know, to the...death and I—"

"The American killed my mother," Nicole said, eyeing me now as if looking for some corroboration of my own nationality. She was blonde and petite and while I didn't know the details of how her mother died, I had to think that Nicole's small stature combined with the fact that *it was her mother*, probably kept her off the suspects list.

"Were you anywhere near when it happened?" I asked.

I looked up at the back of the shop and saw there was a series of second story windows. One of them had curtains in it telling me that the family lived over the shop.

"I was asleep in my bed," Nicole said crossly. "Is that near enough?"

"And you didn't hear anything?"

"What are you suggesting?"

In for a penny. I might as well try to get some answers. It's not like she's going to get any friendlier.

"Just that you were right upstairs when it happened. You didn't hear an argument or your mother, you know...screaming?"

"I couldn't hear anything with that stupid dog barking!"

I looked past Nicole through the open door and into the back of the kitchen where, presumably, the murder had taken place. Had she really just been in there baking and doing the usual stuff less than twelve hours after her mother was murdered? And what dog?

"Was your father upstairs asleep too?"

"Yes, of course, he..." She gave me an even more suspicious look. "Are you with a newspaper?"

Before I had a chance to think about whether I should answer truthfully, a large man filled the doorway behind Nicole. He snarled a garble of French to her and she turned and withdrew without another word.

"Get out," he said to me. "I have called the police."

Well, I was pretty sure that was a lie since nobody had functioning phones any more.

"I'm not trespassing. I'm just taking a walk. Are you Monsieur Ducharme?"

"Who wants to know?" he said, stepping into the alley. I couldn't help taking a few steps back.

"I saw you attack your wife yesterday, Monsieur Ducharme," I said, sounding way more brave than I felt.

"Eh?" The look on his face was almost laughable. That is, unless you were the one standing alone with him in a deserted alley.

"That's right," I said shakily. "I saw you. And then ten hours later she's dead? You don't have to be Stephen Hawking to figure out *that* equation."

"I did not kill Marine," he said vehemently. "You saw nothing."

I really wasn't sure what to say to that. But by the way he was clenching and unclenching his fists, I did think it might be prudent to bring the interview to a close.

"*Nothing*, do you hear?" he said suddenly, reaching out and grabbing me by the shoulders.

"*Help! Help!*" I shrieked, trying to twist out of his grip.

Monsieur Monster dropped his hand from my shoulder and turned to look at the entrance of the alley just in time to see two burly policemen—their billy clubs drawn—headed toward him.

I felt a rush of relief right up until the moment where one cop reached me and yanked me away while the other—I kid you not—*apologized* to the big ape who'd been about to tear me limb from limb.

7

The Short Straw

It appeared that Monsieur Ducharme had indeed called the police before he'd stepped out into the alley. What I had thought were my two knights in shining gabardine were in fact responding to a dispatcher's 911 call.

Or whatever the equivalent to that is in France.

The bad news was that I was going to spend the rest of the day and night in jail courtesy of the Aix *police municipale*.

The good news was that I now knew there was at least limited phone service in Aix.

So yay.

I have to say I have never been arrested before and so the whole experience was somewhat interesting to me and not that uncomfortable. It seemed the police didn't have a suitable place to put me so they locked me in someone's office for the night where I slept on the couch with a blanket.

Since I now knew the police had phone access, I asked for my phone call but they ignored me. They did take my bag with my passport but I must say any "booking" must have happened while I was asleep since I never talked to anyone.

I enjoyed a salad and a delicious Coquilles Saint-Jacques for dinner with a very nice Pouilly Fuisse. It was quiet in the office where they'd put me and after I realized I was indeed under arrest and not going anywhere anytime soon, I used the time to think.

One thing I learned from my conversation with Nicole was that she and her father were both upstairs at the time of the murder. Mind you, since they weren't sleeping together—*one would hope*—neither had an alibi. Which brought me to Monsieur Nose-Puller.

There was no doubt in my mind that he was the murderer.

How could the police not see this? I'm sure I wasn't the only one to notice that he was abusive to Madame Ducharme. On top of that he had means and opportunity.

Why in the world were the police not arresting *him*?

Did he have some kind of special arrangement with the police?

A needle of suspicion penetrated my brain. I knew my country wasn't popular at the moment...but was there a reason why they wanted to pin this murder on the American?

*****

The next morning I was reminded of that joke about how most of us could improve our lot in life by merely committing a serious crime and getting arrested in order to enjoy a lifetime of paid healthcare, three squares and unlimited Internet access.

After a not-at-all-uncomfortable night on the leather couch, I was awakened by a sour faced police attendant with a tray containing the bare basics for living as far as the French are concerned: a piping hot *café crème*, a fresh croissant with butter and the most exquisite strawberry jam I ever tasted, and a glass of freshly squeezed orange juice.

I kid you not.

I was just finishing my breakfast when the attendant came back for the tray accompanied by someone I knew.

"Good morning, Jules," Luc said as he surveyed the room before turning to survey me as well.

The nerve!

"May I help you?" I said coolly.

"It is I who is here to help you, I think," he said with a smile. "Are you ready to leave?"

"Hmmph!" I said, getting up in my best Scarlett O'Hara flounce although granted I didn't have the petticoats to really pull it off. "To the interrogation room, I suppose? Did you bring your thumbscrews?"

He led the way down the hall and out into the bright sunshine of another beautiful day in Aix-en-Provence. His police car sat outside. I was surprised he didn't have the same trouble that Thibault did about people wanting to steal his car. Probably having the word POLICE painted on the side helped.

I got in the car, deliberately not looking at Luc. In fact, looking everywhere except at him. As soon as he got in the driver's seat, I turned on him.

"You just threw my stuff in the street? What right did you have? I thought we were friends!"

He sighed and pulled away from the police station.

"It was *you* without the right to live there and I did not throw your stuff in the street. I have it with me in the back seat."

I glanced in the back and saw my rolling suitcase.

"I thought since Chabanel is so provincial that perhaps you might prefer to relocate to Aix," he said.

I looked at his profile as he drove.

"Am I being run out of town, Sheriff?"

"I do not know this reference," Luc said, clearly uncomfortable with my direct approach. "I can take you to the American Consulate."

"The American Consulate has been closed since the EMP went off. And I think you know that."

He glanced at me then and I swear I saw him flush with embarrassment. He knew he was acting like an ass. The question was, *why was he acting like an ass?*

"I'm staying at the Hotel Cezanne," I said. "You can take me there."

"You have friends there?"

"As a matter of fact, I do. The parents of the man accused of murdering Marine Ducharme."

Luc slammed on the brakes which actually wasn't as dramatic as you might think since he was the only car on the road. But the message was nonetheless delivered effectively.

"*Non*," he said, turning to face me fully in the car. "That is police business."

Without knowing I was going to do it, I hopped out of the car and opened the backseat door and grabbed my bag. Before Luc had a chance to react, I leaned into the passenger's side window to address him.

"Last time I checked, Aix wasn't your jurisdiction," I said.

"I am instructing you not to involve yourself. You will stay away from this case."

"Nice try."

His mouth fell open and I cannot tell you how gratifying *that* was.

"Jules," he said, his face darkening with his mounting anger. "You will not—"

"See ya, *mon capitaine*," I said tossing my hair over my shoulder as I turned on my heel and walked away.

All of which was just so perfect except for the part where I'd been counting on a little help from him in getting a look at Elliott's case file.

8

All Good Things

As soon as Luc drove off I felt as if my last friend in the world had just walked away from me and that's pretty weird since first, *I* was the one who had done the walking and second, Luc was clearly not much of a friend.

I'd been so wrong about him! I thought we had a thing! I mean, we'd never kissed or anything but we'd done plenty of silent communicating, or at least I thought we had.

Obviously I was the only one doing any communicating and not much of that since here's where we both ended up.

So fine. Good to know. Chief Luc DeBray was simply the head of the *police municipale* in Chabanel, a village I no longer belonged to, if I ever had. And honestly, when I calmed down a bit I realized that while it was true I'd expected to be able to stay in the Poupard's apartment until they came back, I had to admit I had no idea of what their situation was back in Atlanta. For all I knew they were homeless now too.

And if you were going to be homeless in an apocalypse, honestly, I think I'll take Aix where they're still serving *petit cafés* and croissants.

I wheeled my bag upstairs to my room at the hotel, nodding at Monsieur Benet who continued to seem totally cool with me roosting in one of his rooms.

"*Bonjour*, Madame Hooker," Monsieur Benet said pleasantly, prompting me once again to ask him to please just call me Jules.

I noticed that a few of the American guests were sitting in the Parisian-style lobby sipping *café crèmes* and flipping through three-month-old English-language magazines.

Once upstairs in my room, I hung up my clothes and smoothed out the wrinkles from my silk blouses and linen slacks the best I could. I didn't know who had collected my things and repacked them but at least they hadn't just jammed them all in the case willy-nilly. I touched a matching bra and panty set and found myself wondering if it was Luc who'd packed them so nicely for me.

Shaking off my momentary pulse of sentimentality, I stripped off my prison garb—the outfit I'd now worn two days in a row—and stepped into the shower where miraculously, there was water pressure.

I have no idea how Aix was doing it, but perhaps being forced to live here wouldn't be so awful after all.

Once I'd washed my hair with the hotel shampoo and conditioner—another bonus over Chabanel—I finger dried it to create haphazard waves around my face. Normally I like more control over my hair and a ton of product and flat irons give me that but the circumstances seemed to warrant a more analog approach and it turned out I rather liked the effect.

Feeling better, I decided it was time to talk to the Whites and see if they had any more information about Elliott. I didn't have anything hopeful to tell them—not with Agnes saying she *wasn't* Elliott's girlfriend and *hadn't* spent the critical night with him. On the other hand, my brief interview with the family of the deceased made me more convinced than ever that

Monsieur Ducharme was the one the police needed to be talking to.

Unfortunately, the fact that they arrested *me* and hauled *me* off to the hoosegow and apologized to *him* when he was clearly laying hands on me made me think that there was some kind of deal between him and the police.

And if that was the case, Elliott was screwed.

I walked down the main staircase—as everyone did now that there was no electricity to run the elevator —and smiled at Monsieur Benet at the counter. He was counting out fat nubs of candles to be distributed to each of our rooms later. Most of us still had flashlights and I hated to think about the coming time when all the batteries were totally dead.

"Jules!" Jim got up from one of the lobby chairs, a grin on his face when he saw me. It was such an infectious expression and made me feel so welcome that I almost nearly sort of forgot all about Luc dumping me and my things in the middle of Aix and speeding back to Chabanel at warp speed.

"You're not going to believe what happened to me," I said, greeting him with a cheek kiss. I looked around to see that Joanne and her husband Barry were also in the lobby but there was no sign of the Whites.

"Jane and Glenn are still up in their room," Jim said as he watched me scan the room. "They went down to the *gendarmerie* and were allowed to see Elliott briefly."

"Hello, darling," Joanne said as she spotted me. "We've been wondering what happened to you."

I smiled at her where she was sitting with Barry. When he looked up from the four-week-old newspaper he seemed fascinated with, I could see the stark line of the fresh scratch etched across his cheek.

❀ ❀ ❀ ❀ ❀

Luc could've kicked himself.

Why hadn't he just told Jules exactly what happened? Why hadn't he just laid it all out that the Poupards' cousins had legitimate papers that made Jules staying on in their apartment legally impossible?

As he drove back to Chabanel, knowing how badly he'd mismanaged all of this, he felt his heart sinking with every mile. A part of him had actually been relieved when Jules decided to go to Aix for what appeared to be an extended stay.

While he personally hated that there was now no chance that he might run into her at the *boulangerie* or the market or even Bar à GoGo, her departure definitely got the mayor off his back.

But *les soeurs* were restless without Jules.

When he'd followed up with the old ladies two days ago, it turned out their complaint had to do with the fact that someone had broken into Jules' apartment. Of course the so-called break-in had been by the rightful owners but that had only enraged the Madame Twins.

Dealing with them on top of the Poupard cousins had not been pleasant.

After that, *les soeurs* had issued a complaint to his office two or three times a day—often walking their charges in to personally present them to him—almost as if in protest. And while Luc knew the sisters were being provided for with food and candles, he also knew they were restless and unhappy without Jules there.

He knew exactly how they felt.

Which was why he'd been elated to receive the call from the Aix police in reference to Jules. He was sure he'd shocked the desk sergeant when he told him he

64

would not only vouch for Madame Hooker but would arrive in Aix to have her released into his custody.

He gunned the car on the empty stretch of highway toward Chabanel.

Somehow it had all sounded so much nicer in theory than in reality.

9

Sowing and Reaping

Honestly, it wasn't just the scratch that bothered me.

It was the look in Barry's eyes that said he had a secret.

An ugly secret.

"Whoa!" I said. "What happened to you?"

Barry touched his face as if only now realizing he had a scratch.

"Oh, this? Nothing. Just got a little too close and personal with a rose bush in the courtyard."

If he could only see his face when he said that he would realize what a bad liar he is, I thought.

I glanced at Joanne on the off chance she might be in on this. But either *she* gave him the scratch in which case it was none of my business or she was clueless. She appeared to totally accept his lie and there was no trace of guilt on her face that might lead anyone to think she'd given it to him.

Barry had a scratch on his face and he's lying about how he got it.

Are you thinking what I'm thinking?

"You all know the Whites have asked me to investigate the case," I said to Joanne and Barry. "I've been meaning to ask everyone where they were the night of the murder."

"You mean so you can pin it on one of *us*?" Joanne said incredulously.

"I'm hoping it will be *pinned* on the person responsible," I said reasonably. "So if you didn't do it or you're not protecting someone who did, you shouldn't have a problem telling me where you were two nights ago."

Before Joanne could respond—and by the look on her face it was going to be a doozy—Jim took me by the arm and pulled me out of the lobby, down the steps and out the front door of the hotel.

I knew I'd gone too far and could only blame my pique over Luc's betrayal and the fact that I hadn't had lunch yet.

"Jules, really?" Jim said with exasperation. "Is this how you make friends?"

"No," I said defensively. "This is how I try to earn a living."

"Can you do it without pissing everyone off?" He ran a hand through his hair and looked totally exasperated. "In the course of normal conversation this morning, both Joanne and Barry mentioned to me that they'd spent the whole of that night alone in their room. They left the café, walked back with all of us to the hotel, and then let themselves into their hotel room which they didn't come out of until the next morning."

"So they say."

"Of course, so they say! But the point is they're each other's alibi, okay?"

"Where did Barry get that scratch on his face?"

"Scratch?"

"Oh, come on! You didn't see it? It wasn't there two nights ago."

He shrugged. "I just need you to be mindful of the things you say. We expats have to stick together."

"Maybe we do," I said. "And maybe we don't."

I don't know why I was being such a pill because the fact was I was pretty much stuck in Aix now and Jim was right that all these people would be *my* people

—as surprisingly distasteful as I suddenly found that thought to be.

"Look, I've got a few errands to run," Jim said. "Why don't we meet this evening for an *apero*? Sound good? Then you can tell me where you were last night."

That sounded reasonable and as I watched him stride down the street toward the Cours Mirabeau I reminded myself that I was not homeless nor was I friendless.

And regardless of how badly Luc clearly wanted me out of Chabanel I would find a way—probably through Thibault—to get back at least once in awhile to check on the Madame Twins.

With this plan comforting me somewhat, I walked toward the Cours Mirabeau, enjoying the feeling of the sun on my hair, and delighted with the fact that it wouldn't frizz as a result—unlike its natural tendency in Atlanta.

I was officially starving since I'd become unfortunately used to regular meals ever since I landed in France and now couldn't go three hours without one. One of the many reasons why Aix was superior to Chabanel of course was the plenitude of bakeries and sandwich stands.

I went to the first *sandwiche* stand I found and bought a half baguette stuffed with ham, pickles, tomato slices and thick wedges of Brie. Then I found a nice park bench to enjoy my lunch and watch the world pass me by.

I didn't know what Aix was like *before* the bomb dropped but I could hardly imagine it was more charming than it was now. Of course, things typically got a whole lot less charming after dark without electricity but for the moment, everything was lovely.

One thing I realized about this case was that my two leading theories were that either Monsieur Ducharme killed his wife but was being protected by the police or Elliott really *did* do it—neither which served me very well at all. One, because if Ducharme was being protected by the cops, I'd never be able to unstick them from Elliott and two, if Elliott really did do it, well, I was probably not going to get paid.

I threw my paper napkins and sandwich wrapping in the nearby trash receptacle wondering how the city was paying its garbage men these days but grateful that they were and decided that a *pain au chocolat* was the perfect way to finish my lunch.

With Ducharme's closed, I walked down the first pedestrian street off the Cours Mirabeau until I came to a bakery that looked a lot like Ducharme's only without the great location. This one was called La Bouche—which means *the mouth* in English and which I thought was probably someone's attempt to be witty and fresh but somehow just came off oafish.

But there was nothing oafish about the sweet offerings displayed to majestic delight in the store window. Not unlike Ducharme's, La Bouche knew that the appearance of abundance in their buns and sweet tarts was very alluring. I don't know why that is, but trust me, they nailed it.

Inside there were three people behind the counter —again with the silver tongs—only this time they seemed a whole lot more cheerful. They were all smiling as if they were thoroughly enjoying bestowing their lush confections on their customers. The whole atmosphere was palpable and dramatically different from Ducharme's.

I bought two *pain au chocolats* from a young man with an arm covered with tattoos and an infectious grin.

"English?" he said as he rang up my purchases.

"American," I said. "How did you know I wasn't French?"

He just laughed and after a moment, I did too. As I left the bakery I noticed the woman behind me waiting her turn had a little poodle on a leash. And behind her was a man in a suit squinting into the display case trying to make up his mind and holding a sleepy Yorkie in his arms.

What is it with the French and their dogs? I couldn't help think. Do they truly just bring them everywhere they go? But then I pulled my first warm and flaky pastry out of the bag, my mouth watering in anticipation, I really couldn't think of anything else.

❀ ❀ ❀ ❀ ❀

The watcher leaned against the wide trunk of the plane tree as the American woman ate her pastry on the bench. His fingers moved methodically and rhythmically, unconsciously sprinkling a faint dusting of flour on the ground around him as he watched her.

He felt his agitation throb and grow and he was suddenly very thirsty.

Would she go to the police? Would they believe her? Why couldn't she leave it alone? What was Marine to her?

As he watched her he found certain uncomfortable thoughts developing in his mind and then flitting away as quickly as they'd formed.

Thoughts that nowadays the American tourists were unprotected.

Even last week, one was found dead in an alley and the police merely shrugged. There was no international scrutiny to be concerned with now. No foreign authority to answer to.

He rubbed his hands on his trousers.

One more dead American would not be noticed.

10

Sip Sliding Away

Two cases of vandalism—both of them committed by children.

One case of domestic abuse—a repeat offender and no chance the wife would bring charges.

One case of stolen chocolate truffles.

Luc rubbed his eyes and tossed down the ledger.

The mayor wanted another town hall meeting. The posters and handbills were everywhere around the village—like the announcement of a village *fête*. Beaufait had even gone so far as to print colorful tea towels in lavender and orange to present her event as celebratory and festive as possible.

And of course he would need to stand behind her looking like some idiot country version of secret service —complete with sunglasses and dark blazer, his hands clasped behind his back.

He groaned. Not tonight. Any night but tonight.

He didn't know why he felt that way. Tonight was no different from any other night. Work all day—unless he was working the night shift which he did more and more these days—then fall into bed when it was more morning that night, sleep for a few hours and do it all again.

Is this a life?

"Chief?" Eloise called from the other room. She appeared in his doorway. "Adrien went home sick."

Great. There went Luc's one hope of palming off this town hall meeting on Matteo so he could get out of town.

Before the thought had finished forming in his mind, Luc realized he'd been thinking of escape on some level more or less all day long.

He needed to get back to Aix and talk to Jules. At least tell her how the apartment ended up lost and how sorry he was about that. *And perhaps to ask her how she is doing?*

The more he thought about it the more he realized he needed to do exactly that.

I have been a dolt! And why? Because the mayor doesn't enjoy having an American stranded in her village?

"Chief?" Eloise said. "You okay?"

Luc looked up and frowned. Eloise couldn't handle the town meeting on her own. Perhaps she might've before the EMP but the new order of things had thrown her.

"Where is Romeo?" he asked. Romeo Remey was in his early seventies and officially retired from the *gendarmerie*. But he still helped out from time to time.

"Visiting his sister in Orange," Eloise said.

That settled it.

Luc stood up and grabbed his jacket.

"*Bon.* Sergeant," he said, feeling better than he had in weeks, "you will need to accompany the mayor to the town hall meeting tonight."

He didn't need to look at Eloise's face to see the shock and fear there and so he didn't look. Eloise was in her mid-twenties and had been doing the job for five years. Time to step up.

Time for *everyone* to step up, he thought fiercely.

❉ ❉ ❉ ❉ ❉

I have to say I think I love Aix at dusk the very best.

It already had a major glow going on because of all the golden limestone buildings everywhere but you know eight out of ten artists can't all be wrong: the light in Provence is magical. And for me, that's even truer when I'm sitting at a table with a champagne spritzer in front of me and the world walking by.

Having lived in the commune of Aix for six years, Jim knew Aix pretty well so he picked the café but honestly I don't see how you could go wrong with any of them.

I'd had most of the afternoon to reconsider my bluntness with Joanne and Barry and while I still wasn't satisfied with Barry's answer about how he got his scratch, I had to admit that I'd come on too strong.

Seeing it from their point of view I can see there are few moments more insulting than having a near stranger accuse you of murder.

So I could see why Jim hadn't been impressed with my behavior this morning.

Wait until I tell him I spent the night in jail. I glanced at him between sips and decided that probably wasn't a necessary part of this evening's events.

"You look more relaxed," Jim said with a smile as he lifted his beer to his lips.

Now tell me that's not an insult when someone says that to you. It's on the same level as *you don't look as fat as you did yesterday.* Or *did you do something special with your hair?* when in fact all you did was wash it.

But I just smiled sweetly and sipped my champagne.

As we sat there watching the light slowly leech from the sky in variegated shades of scarlet and gold and finally dark blue, a work detail of four men made its way painstakingly down the Cours Mirabeau.

"What in the world are they doing?" I asked as the workers—dressed in uniform city overalls—climbed long ladders to reach the tops of the street lights.

"They're making sure the street lights will work when they put the generator on," Jim said.

I took in a quick intake of breath and looked at the workers with new appreciation.

"That'll be so beautiful once there's light again," I said.

"As long as we don't run out of fuel."

"They must think there'll be enough, right?"

Jim regarded me with a smile. Talk about relaxed, *Jim* seemed pretty chill tonight too.

"It'll be nice to stroll the Cours Mirabeau again after dark," he agreed.

"More importantly, the cafés and restaurants will be able to stay open later."

"Right. Which is probably more to the point."

I cocked my head and observed him. He was handsome and he was mysterious.

"What brought you to Provence?" I asked as I sipped my drink.

He shrugged so he'd definitely gotten that whole French not-going-to-answer-right-away thing down pat.

"Came here two years ago with my girlfriend," he said.

"Really."

He grinned. "We broke up. She went home. I decided to stay."

"You don't need to work?"

"You just come right out with it, don't you?" But he laughed. "I have a trust fund."

"How does that work now? Can you get to your money?"

"I'd transferred a large chunk of it to the French banks, so to answer your question, yes. At least for the foreseeable future."

I could see he wasn't bothered by my asking him such personal questions. That boded well for the future of our friendship.

"Everyone in Aix still seems to be accepting money," I said, watching a couple leave the café after depositing a few coins on the table. "When will that stop?"

"I'm not sure it will. The banks are still open. The government is still paying their workers in chits or cash. While there'll inevitably be some bartering in the new world, there are many who think cash will have a larger role than previously figured."

"I wonder if the Whites will pay me in cash." I looked at Jim. "What if all their cash is in American banks?"

"I don't know, Jules."

"How can they pay me if their money is in America?"

"I'm sure they wouldn't have offered you the job if they didn't think they could pay you."

"Really, Jim? Do you know *anything* about desperate people? I think they'd have promised me the crown jewels if I'd agree to help them."

"I don't know, Jules."

Yeah, I could see I was working myself up again. And while it was true Jim was paying for the drinks, I didn't want to rely on alcohol to sweeten my normally prickly personality.

Or at least get a reputation for needing it.

"I'm sure it'll all work out," I forced myself to say cheerfully. "Meanwhile, can I use you to bounce some ideas off?"

He signaled to the waiter to bring another round. "Sure, I guess."

"Did you know that Madame Ducharme's husband, Fritz, has a history of abuse?"

I didn't know that for a fact but I thought it was a pretty safe bet.

"You think her husband killed her?" Jim asked.

"You always look at the spouse first! And *this* spouse is an abuser. It is very suspicious to me that the cops aren't looking at him. Plus he has no alibi!"

"How do you know that?"

I waved away the question. "I just know. And are you seriously telling me you didn't see that scratch on Barry? A scratch that he lied about how he got?"

"He did? How do you know that?"

I leaned back in my chair. The workmen were now working in the dark using flashlights to finish their work.

How do you tell someone that you just have a gut feeling? Or that some liars broadcast the fact that they're lying? How do you tell someone who doesn't know that on his own? Of course I also remembered that Jim had lied to me a few weeks ago about something very important.

And I'd hadn't known it was a lie. Which, note to self, meant Jim was a good liar.

Thinking about Lilou Basso's murder last month made me think about Luc and I'd been so good all day staying away from that topic. But the combination of the lovely drink and the warm breeze on a summer night on a French patio all came together to remind me that at one time I'd thought Luc was special.

And I thought he'd felt the same.

"*Bonsoir*," a familiar deep voice called out. "I thought I might find you here."

Before I knew what was happening, Jim was standing up to shake hands with someone who'd approached our table and as soon as Jim moved aside, I saw that it was none other than Luc DeBray himself.

I must have looked drunk at that point because my mouth dropped open.

So amazed was I that Luc was actually standing here in front of me after I'd been thinking of him that I missed the fact that my heart was beating faster and I was having trouble catching my breath. I also missed the part where Jim asked Luc to join us because the next thing I knew Luc was pulling up a chair at the table.

"I am only staying a moment," he said in that velvety tone of his. "I wanted to make sure that you were all right, Jules."

It must have been the two glasses of champagne but I nearly cried when he said that. And then just as quickly I remembered how I'd made certain assumptions and rushed things with my ex-almost-fiancé Gilbert and look how *that* ended up.

"I'm more than all right, as you can see," I said, waving to encompass my situation with Jim at the table. I'm not sure what I was trying to do beyond deliver the message that I wasn't upset or caring about him or Chabanel. That I had *moved on*.

But oh my goodness he did look fine this evening. So French with his unkempt flop of very black hair, his leather jacket over jeans, his dark, dark eyes and thick lashes.

"I wanted you to know you should not worry about *les soeurs*," he said. "They are being fed and I am keeping a close eye on them."

"And my cat?" I blurted.

"Eh?" Luc looked at me in confusion.

"Neige," I said, all of a sudden feeling very sentimental about the cat. "Who's feeding poor Neige?"

Luc looked at Jim as if this were some kind of joke or riddle but Jim just shrugged.

"I will ask after Neige," Luc said. I saw that he was about to leave, having discharged his mission, and a part of me couldn't bear to see him go.

"Okay," I said. "Thanks for dropping by."

Luc hesitated and then shook hands with Jim and gave me a nod. Always before it would have been a cheek kiss. Then he turned and disappeared into the dark.

It was literally ten minutes later before I realized that this must have been Luc's night off and he'd come to Aix looking to spend it with me.

11

The Sweet By and By

So that's that.

What a fool I was to think Jules felt as I do, Luc thought to himself. Just looking at her hanging all over Jim Anderson had told him everything he should have already known.

As he drove way too fast down the D7N toward Chabanel, Luc realized that Jules was exactly where she needed to be. In a bigger city with her own kind. Not just Jim although Luc could see they were a perfect match, but with other Americans.

Let's face it. She was never going to learn to speak French. Or stop trying to find her way back to America. Or accept her new situation.

I must have lost my damn mind.

And now I will go back to Chabanel where there is now no trace of her and I will focus only on the needs of the village.

And somehow thinking that just made him feel so much worse.

❈ ❈ ❈ ❈ ❈

The next morning revealed another exquisite day in the south of France. Blue cloudless skies, a gentle breeze married beautifully with the hot sun, and not a speck of humidity to foul up a girl's impulsive inclination to wear her hair down instead of pinned in a topknot on her head.

After drinks and dinner with Jim last night I decided it was wise to make an early night of it. It hadn't taken me too long to register the feeling that regardless of the fact that Luc had kicked me out of my Chabanel apartment, I'd been disappointed to see him walk away last night.

And annoyed. Because I was afraid he'd jumped to the wrong conclusion and thought I had a thing with Jim. I mean, if it made him jealous that was one thing but I didn't see that tendency in Luc. If anything, he'd probably just leave the playing field.

So annoying!

I'd spent a good part of the night wondering if the Madame Twins really had just shrugged me off that easily and if they were in fact being taken care of. Those two were extremely high maintenance and it was difficult to believe that a couple of city care packages would sort them out. I hoped Luc was doing what he said he was and was actually interacting with them.

Those old broads took a *serious* amount of interacting, trust me.

When I came down to the lobby the next morning I thought that Joanne and Barry must be holed up in their room since they were nowhere to be seen. Jim told me last night that poor Jane and Glenn were spending most of their time loitering around the *police municipale* hoping to talk to their son. He said they'd hired a French lawyer who didn't speak English so I wasn't sure how well any of that was going.

Since as far as I knew I was still on the job, I decided to try to talk to Nicole Ducharme again. After that, I was thinking of going to the police station myself to see if I could wheedle any info out of the stick-up-his-butt detective on the case.

Just thinking of that guy made me think of Luc—not because Luc is uptight, although I can't definitely say he isn't—but because I couldn't help but think that Luc was my best bet for getting my hands on the case file or at the very least basic information on the murder.

I still didn't even know exactly how Madame Ducharme died!

As this was a Thursday the twice-a-week flea market was set up on the east side of Cours Mirabeau. I took my time walking past the tables laden with various market delights like lavender honey in vintage bottles, vibrant kitchen linens and tablecloths in color block hues of lilac, blue and pink, as well as towers of woven straw hats in every style and size.

One of the tables featured pyramid stacks of Marseille soaps in at least a dozen colors in their famous square block shapes. And while I did see a little bit of bartering going on, for the most part, everyone was paying in cash.

Were they paying in cash back in Atlanta? I wondered, or had they figured out a different method? An image of people heaving bricks through the downtown Macy's store window came to mind.

I walked straight to La Bouche and bought an almond croissant. Once again I saw customers who felt comfortable bringing their dogs into the bakery and marveled that everyone was okay with this.

The cute tattoo guy slipped an extra croissant into my bag, and at one point, he turned to look over his shoulder and spoke to someone named Cocoa. When I followed his gaze, I saw that he was talking to a little black dog sitting on a cushion in the doorway between the back rooms and the show room.

Hello? French Health Department much?

I ate my croissant as I walked away and absentmindedly ran a finger around the waistband of my linen slacks to remind myself that I probably couldn't tolerate this high-carb lifestyle too much longer without dire consequences.

I sat on a park bench to finish off my breakfast and enjoy the slow ebb and flow of the morning. While Aix was much more energetic than Chabanel it hadn't taken me long to register how easy-going the pace really was. From where I sat I could see that *Les Deux Garcons Café* —the restaurant that had opened in 1792—was doing a brisk breakfast business. Next to it was a boarded up ATM machine, a pizzeria and what used to be a Rolex store, also boarded up.

I'd done a good job of keeping Luc out of my head so far this morning—I find sugar helps—and now I needed to rouse myself and earn my keep.

I stood up and brushed the flakes of pastry from my lap. As I made my way toward Ducharme's it struck me that a good reason *why* the crime scene tape maybe wasn't still up—if it ever had been—was because the Aix cops didn't *need* to learn what the scene had to tell them.

And *that* was because they already knew who they were arresting.

I know I'm starting to sound paranoid but it was frankly the only explanation I could come up with for why the cops hadn't arrested the most obvious man for the crime—Fritz Ducharme.

Or maybe now that criminal investigators don't have forensics help they simply don't know how to process a post-apocalyptic crime scene?

As I approached Ducharme's I saw that a sign had been added to the front of the store which read *Fermé* or Closed.

As if somebody couldn't figure that out by the dark blinds pulled down the front display window.

In any case since there was no hope of my examining the crime scene, I thought I might at least have a snoop around the back alley that led to the entrance of the rear kitchen. I wasn't really expecting much but then I hadn't expected much that time I went rooting around my back garden looking for clues on who killed poor Lilou either.

And I'd found a major clue that had led to her killer.

Buoyed by this encouraging if unlikely possibility, I turned down the narrow alley just in time to see the door to the kitchen slowly close.

I stopped and stared for just a moment and then as quietly as I could I ran to where the door had closed but the latch hadn't clicked shut.

Someone had just gone in the kitchen. I looked around the alley with its seven-foot stone walls. They must have gone in because they sure as heck hadn't just come out. There was no place for them to go except the way I'd just come.

With my heart pounding in two-time, I put my hand on the doorknob and slowly pulled the kitchen door open, praying there would be no tell-tale accompanying creak.

There wasn't.

What there was when I opened the door just wide enough to slip through I could see a man standing over a desk and going through its open drawers.

There were two tables placed end to end to form prep stations. Ducharme's specialized in small, hand-crafted confections. This must be where the magic happened. There were table top cookers and what looked like chocolate molding workstations as well as cooling tables with mesh grids and cutters in all shapes.

A large copper vat sat at the end of the farthest table with a gigantic thermometer attached to the side of it. I crept closer to the vat to look inside and saw that it was full of a dark golden batter of some kind. The flecks of dust and debris on the surface told me this concoction was not fresh. My guess would be that Madame Ducharme had been working on or near it at the time of her murder.

My eye caught the glimmer of something metallic in the mesh strainer hooked to the side and half submerged in what I now detected to be melted caramel.

This was the crime scene! That could be a clue related to the murder!

I was so excited that without thinking I reached out to touch the mesh catcher.

Unfortunately, I hadn't seen the beaker of vanilla that was perched on an inside shelf of the vat. My hand bumped it and the beaker began to wobble. Honestly, if I hadn't yelped in dismay I might well have caught the beaker, retrieved what I could now see was a heavy gold ring caught in the mesh, and beat it out the door with no one the wiser.

But yeah, that's not what happened.

Cursing and juggling with the stupid beaker, I saw the man out of the corner of my eye turn to me in surprise just as the glass beaker went crashing to the floor, breaking into a thousand shards.

"*Qui êtes vous?*" the man asked in a deep but not unfriendly voice.

"Whatever you said goes double for me," I said, backing away from the broken mess on the floor and forcing myself not to look at the mesh trap. The last thing I needed was for him to see what I was after.

"American?" He said it with a turn of his head as if examining me like I was a curious specimen of some kind.

"The bigger question," I said, "is who are *you* and what are you doing here?"

He grinned and patted his pockets before retrieving a business card and handing it to me. The card read *Albert Bliss La Bouche Pâtisserie.*

"You work at La Bouche?" I asked.

"I own La Bouche," he said as the returned to his examination of the desk.

I saw that he was rifling through a small box of recipes. He was stealing Madame Ducharme's secret recipes! Not that I knew they were secret recipes but if they were, he was stealing them!

"I see what you're doing!" I said. "You can't break in here and take those."

He tucked a notecard into his pocket and turned to me with a genuinely curious look in his eye now.

"Marine always promised me her French salted caramel chocolate tart."

"Says you."

"Yes, of course says me." He shook his head and grinned. "You Americans. It is like watching a western on television. Always amusing."

"If she really said you could have the recipe then why didn't you just knock on the front door and ask for it?" I was sure I had him on the ropes now. Even if, maddeningly, he didn't appear at all flustered.

"Unlike you, that is exactly what he did," Nicole said as she moved into the kitchen from the front selling room. She must have been listening to the entire exchange.

"*Maman* wanted Monsieur Bliss to have the caramel chocolate tart and I let him in to get the recipe. *You* however I did not."

I glanced at the back door. If he came in the front, then how come...?

"I stepped outside for a smoke," Bliss said with a shrug, answering my unspoken question. Then he turned to Nicole and the two embraced and he kissed her on both cheeks. He murmured something low to her in French that sounded a whole lot like his sympathies and she thanked him before he turned to leave.

As he passed me, he tapped his breast pocket where the recipe card was and gave me a wink.

I guess I'd be jolly too if I made chocolate tarts and beignets all day long.

As soon as he left I turned to Nicole.

"Look, I'm sorry," I said. "I thought he'd broken into your place."

Nicole waved away my words as if she were too weary to deal with them.

"Please just go."

"I will, of course. I just have one question and then I swear I'll never bother you again."

"What is it?" she said with exasperation. "What is your question?"

"Why do you think Elliott White killed your mother? What in the world was his motive?"

Nicole sagged to a sitting position in the desk chair and her eyes stared in a glaze at the kitchen equipment as if wondering what in the world she would do with it all now.

"My mother shocked him."

"Shocked him? How?"

Nicole pinched the skin between her eyes together as if trying to dissipate a headache. Then she looked at me. "You have spoken to Agnes Valentin?"

"Elliott's girlfriend? Yes."

"*Not* his girlfriend," Nicole said firmly. "When Agnes broke up with him, she did not tell him why. So

88

when Elliott came to my mother to demand she give Agnes her job back—"

"Wait. Your mother fired Agnes?"

Nicole shrugged. "Agnes is a sweet girl but she was a sloppy worker. Not at all Ducharme's brand."

If true, this did not help my client, I couldn't help but think.

"So Elliott came to ask for Agnes's job back," I prompted Nicole.

"*Ordered* her to give it back! But not before sending *Maman* a threatening note that he would make sure no one ever shopped at Ducharme's again if she didn't. Did you know that? He wrote that he would personally put a brick through the front window!"

I have to say it was probably asking too much not to have a client who wasn't a douche bag. It was probably all that I could hope for that they paid my bill. Oh yeah, and that they're innocent.

"Go on," I said, beginning to feel my own headache coming on.

"When Elliott White came here that night, my mother told him the real reason Agnes broke up with him."

"Which was?"

"Because she was in love with me."

I stared at Nicole for a moment.

"So you're saying your mother hit Elliott with the truth bomb and it went off all over her."

"I have no idea what you just said."

"How is it you heard this exchange between your mother and Elliott but you *didn't* hear your mother's screams a few minutes later?"

"I have answered your *one* question and now you will please leave as I am sure the Aix police are much harsher the second time around with repeat offenders."

89

12

Nothing Ventured

I had to get back inside that kitchen.

It was all I could think of. Once I'd seen that ring glimmering in the caramel mesh net, I couldn't get it out of my head that it was somehow germane to the murder.

And why wouldn't it be?

Since the cops clearly hadn't processed the crime scene worth a damn, it made total sense that there was evidence left behind with the killer's mark on it. And while there was no longer any way to pull DNA off it, there were still other ways to prove who it belonged to.

I'm not a hundred per cent what those ways were but I'm sure they existed.

As I hurried past the flea market tables and the temporary socca booths back to the Hotel Cezanne, I couldn't help but think that my conversation with Nicole changed everything.

She had intimated that she'd heard a conversation between her mother and Elliott—which sounded about right if Nicole had been in the bedroom overhead. But she also said she hadn't heard the murder happening.

So either Nicole was lying to protect someone—her father?— or the two events happened at two separate times.

With two separate people.

So now the big question was: *Who else visited Madame Ducharme that night*?

The hotel was quiet and the front desk vacant when I got back and I glad for that. While Monsieur Benet had sort of joked about wanting me to find his dog in exchange for my room I got the unmistakable impression that he really did think I would be out looking for the animal.

By the time I got back to my room I'd decided that I needed to go back to the Béchamel *pâtisserie* after dark. I needed to break in and *get that ring* trapped in the caramel mesh. And while I was there I needed to do the crime scene processing that I was now positive the police hadn't done.

I wasn't completely sure what I'd do with my findings beyond my fantasy of laying them out dramatically before the entire Aix police force and having everyone fall all over themselves marveling at my brilliant detective work.

As I changed clothes and got ready for my night's escapade, I couldn't help think how so much of what I learned today was not good for Elliott.

So Agnes is gay? I certainly hadn't picked up on *that* and while it's true Elliott was more or less a tool I'm not sure even I could be convinced to turn gay in order to avoid dating him.

But that wasn't the main take-away. The main take-away was that if Nicole was telling the truth and Elliott got the news about Agnes from Madame Béchamel, that might well have been a big enough shock to trigger an attack.

Oh, crap. Am I really trying to prove the innocence of a murderer? And what am I going to tell the Whites? There's probably no way they're going to pay me for confirming their son's guilt.

As I was reapplying my makeup to make it less reflective in the dark, I couldn't get over how cool and collected Nicole had been today. While tired looking, she didn't appear to be in mourning at all. And giving away her mother's recipes? Did she not intend to continue running the bakery?

And then there was the question of whether the bakery belonged to Fritz now that Marine was dead? But without Marine, who would make the amazing confections?

I got a mental picture of Fritz and for a moment I stopped applying my peach blush.

If I was caught tonight things could get ugly. Fritz was unstable and violent. That much I knew.

He was also very likely a cold-blooded killer.

❉ ❉ ❉ ❉ ❉

Jane White sat at the stone table in the hotel courtyard and stared at her hands, trying to stay calm, trying to get her thoughts in order. Glenn sat beside her, drumming his fingers on the table as his eyes darted rapidly all around.

The police had let them see Elliott today but only for a few moments. Elliott had wept and railed, protested his innocence and begged his parents to get him released.

Jane covered her face with her hands as if to blot out the memory.

"We'll get him out," Glenn said unenthusiastically.

She glanced at him. He looked as if he'd aged ten years since they'd been stranded in this God-forsaken country.

"How?" she said, hating the plaintiveness in her voice. "Even our lawyer doesn't seen hopeful."

"Who can tell what that guy thinks?" Glenn said. "I didn't understand a single word he said."

"Jim offered to come and translate for us," Jane said, hearing her voice rise in pitch.

"We don't need the world knowing our business."

Jane stared at him as if seeing him for the first time. They'd been married thirty-one years. Had she ever really known him?

"You left in the middle of the night," she said suddenly. "The night of the murder."

He looked at her then, his expression surprised and...was that fear?

"No, I didn't," he said, twisting the wedding ring on his hand.

"I saw you."

"I just went to get some air. Jane, don't look at me like that. More than ever, we have to stick together! Surely you can see that?"

She turned away. Of course he would say that. Of course he would. After all, that's what anyone would say who didn't have an alibi.

❀❀❀❀❀

I dressed in black jeans and matching blue-black ballet flats and slipped out of the hotel clutching only a small flashlight and a credit card that was otherwise totally useless these days. I hadn't gotten a good look at the lock on the Ducharme bakery door—either front or back—but I'd rather have the card and need it than curse the fact that I'd left it behind.

As I crept out the front door of the hotel, I saw the empty food and water bowl for Monsieur Benet's still-missing dog Beignet. God knows what happened to her. I crossed my fingers and hoped she'd found a good home.

It was a moonless night, which worked in my favor. The new street lamps which had been such a thrill just a few hours ago, were a definite negative tonight. Fortunately, to save fuel in the generators, the street lamps were switched off at midnight and so I hurried down the cobblestone streets in almost complete darkness toward the Coeur Mirabeau.

All I knew was that I *had* to look around that kitchen! It might reveal nothing or it might be the single most important thing that helped prove Elliott's innocence.

Naturally, if I got caught—well, best not go down that road. I used to ride horses in competition when I was a teenager and my trainer always told me that half the work to achieving success was what happened in your mind. If you saw yourself sailing cleanly over all the jumps in the ring, than barring something unforeseen, you would.

Likewise, if you thought the horse would balk or you'd fall, you just guaranteed yourself a trip to the emergency room.

Lovely woman, Frau Taylor, my trainer. I wonder what little children she was chopping up back in Atlanta to keep herself fed during the apocalypse.

Coeur Mirabeau had been full of dogs just a few hours ago —some on leashes and some not—but now there was nothing.

Would somebody be out walking their dog in the pitch dark? Was that believable?

I reached the Ducharme *pâtisserie* and waited at the street corner, watching it for a moment to make sure there was nobody around. Then keeping close to the side of the building I walked to the front of the bakery.

I went to the front door but saw immediately that my credit card would be no match for its lock. Disappointed but not discouraged, I hurried down the side alley to the back of the bakery.

I stood at the back door and fished out the card. It was so quiet tonight I felt like I could hear my own heart beating.

I knew I needed to get in and out quickly. I glanced at the window over the back door—Nicole's bedroom. It was darkened. Where was Fritz's room? For a moment, I hesitated.

Did I really need to do this? Did I really have to see inside?

But I knew I did. Without *some* piece of evidence, I had absolutely nothing. Without a clue or even an idea of where to go next, all I had was the idea of trying to string up poor Barry Simpson for having a run-in with a rose bush and hoping the cops didn't decide to take him *and* Elliott too. Besides—big fat liar or not—I had my heart set on the murderer being Fritz.

The card slipped easily between the door and the doorjamb. I slid the card around until I felt it slip under the angled end of the bolt. The lock clicked open. Even though I knew there wouldn't be an alarm sounding, I held my breath as I eased the door open.

I stepped into the kitchen, my heart pounding like a drill hammer now that I was actually in.

First—*get the ring out of the caramel vat.*

I used my flashlight to cut through the darkness so I wouldn't bring down a shelf full of ceramic mixing bowls or worse. I walked to the copper vat and shone my beam into the batter. Instantly I saw the ring. Without worrying about needing to preserve fingerprints or DNA, I reached in and plucked it out, wiping some of the goo off on my jeans and then tucking the ring into my pocket.

I listened but heard absolutely nothing.

A part of me was screaming in my head: *You got it, now get out!*

But unfortunately there's always that other part of me. You know the one. I think they call it the *hold my beer watch this* one.

But in any case, I couldn't help but think *I'm here at great personal risk so I need to make the most of it.*

I flashed the light along the wall of shelves of clear glass containers filled with row after row of nonpareils, sanding sugar in a rainbow of colors, candied ginger, shredded coconut, chocolate bits in sizes ranging from tiny to as big as my thumb, colored sprinkles, candied cherries and chopped nuts.

I played the flashlight beam on the desktop which I thought was very tidy for a work desk. Since I didn't know what I was looking for—nor even if I was seeing something out of place—I told myself *three minutes and then you leave.*

I stepped further into the room and passed the light over the shelves of white bowls in every size. Molds, baking pans, springform pans and cupcake tins lined the other shelves. It looked like a warehouse of a major kitchen supply store. With everything positioned so perfectly it was hard to believe that these items were actually used on a daily basis. Madame Ducharme must have been a majorly compulsive order freak.

And then I saw it.

The thing that shouldn't have been there.

It wasn't eye level to an average sized cop—if indeed they'd even bothered to process this room—but it jumped right out at me.

The corner of a white envelope tucked between two fat white bowls on the shelf.

I took a step forward and touched the envelope before gingerly pulling it out.

The envelope had the logo of the Hotel Cezanne on it.

Was this the envelope that had held Elliott's threatening note? But no, I could feel there was something inside.

Anybody else would have pocketed the envelope to examine it later at her leisure some place safe.

It's called delayed gratification and trust me, I'm very bad at it.

I had to know what was in that envelope right then. I tucked the flashlight under my arm so that I could open the envelope without dropping it. The envelope was unsealed so I was able to easily pry out of it the folded banker's check that was inside.

The first thing I saw on the check was the name of an American bank. The second thing was the amount. Ten thousand US dollars and it was written out to *Marine Ducharme*.

On the date of the murder.

I was so excited I could barely hold the flashlight still. I glanced at the signature line to see the fourth and biggest surprise.

It was signed by Barry Simpson.

Holy moley! He'd been here that night! He'd given Madame Ducharme ten thousand dollars the night she was murdered! Was she blackmailing him? Was this a bribe? Did anyone check to see if it was *Barry's* skin underneath her fingernails?

My heartbeat was racing and I felt a warmth radiating throughout my body.

I'd just found the evidence I needed to free Elliott. I was so excited I was speed racing in my mind as I imagined the expressions on Jane and Glenn's faces when I showed them this check and they realized that their son was about to be released *all thanks to me*.

What an amazing, wonderfully fantastic feeling!

"Who's there?" Fritz's voice boomed out.

13

Make it or Break it

Thanking God and all the saints for the fact that I'd left the back door open, I pivoted on one foot and bolted for the door, knocking down three cookie sheets whose edges were sticking out too far off shelves in the process.

Through the din of bakeware crashing to the floor I heard a steady stream of French being screamed behind me as if it were the soundtrack to my own personal nightmare.

If Fritz got his hands on me I was dead.

Literally. Dead.

I reached the door just as I heard him lumber down my path through the carnage of cake pans and molds with dishes and ceramic cake stands that were tumbling to the floor in his wake.

Get out! My brain screamed at me.

He had longer legs. He was fueled by fury and indignation.

My own fear served more to weaken me than energize me. That was the thought I had as I felt an iron hand clamp down on my shoulder. The pain shot through my neck and up into my skull.

Fritz jerked me around to face him and I dropped my flashlight. I began to lose my balance and flailed my arms to stay upright. His grip on me was the only thing that kept me standing.

"Papa?" Nicole's voice came down the hallway.

The second Fritz hesitated at the sound of Nicole's voice, I twisted out of his grasp and shot out the open door.

I ran down the alley but by the time I reached the main street I could tell he wasn't following me.

Probably busy dialing the Aix police station.

My shoulder throbbed from his vice-like grip as I made my way back to the hotel in the dark, not at all sure if tonight had been a success or a disaster.

Once back at the hotel, I stripped off my clothes and changed into my silk baby doll pjs. I hated to be caught in something so vulnerable when the police showed up but it was either that or look like a cat burglar and I was pretty sure the Aix police were totally into jumping to conclusions.

I crawled into bed, shaking.

If the American Consulate had been open I would have gone there. I have never felt more alone or more vulnerable and unprotected in my entire life. I knew the police were coming—on the word of a murderer—and I knew they wouldn't believe my story over his.

Keeping in mind, of course, that my story was a lie. *But still!*

I lay in the darkened hotel room and listened for the sound of hobnail boots coming pounding up the stairs to arrest me—*and possibly take me to the Place des Martrys?*—until finally the exhaustion of the night and the stress of my fears all came together to trump my overactive imagination and I drifted off to sleep.

❀ ❀ ❀ ❀ ❀

The next morning, I woke up, astonished that the police hadn't come for me after all. The sun peeked in through the curtains of my hotel window and I realized I was hungry.

After showering and popping an ibuprofen that I found in my luggage for the ache in my shoulder where that psycho had grabbed me last night, I dressed in a simple knit dress and sandals.

I tucked the ring and the check into my favorite Kate Spade hobo bag with twenty euros which was all I had left —maybe it was time to ask the Whites for an advance?— and went down to breakfast.

The hotel's breakfast room was a sunny and tidily furnished room with flowers on all the tables. I chose a table nearest a window that overlooked the hotel's private courtyard. A young woman in a starched apron brought me a coffee and a croissant without my having to ask. I found myself wondering again how everyone was getting paid these days.

Once I felt the dark magic of the espresso coursing through my veins, I slathered the croissant with butter and jam and polished it off in three bites. So much for savoring my food. I will never be French in that way. If something's good, I want it all and I want it now.

Two other people came into the breakfast room. I didn't know them but I knew they were stranded tourists like everyone else. They had that uniformly stunned look on their faces. I assumed they were nonEuropeans since it would be much easier to go back home if you were German or Italian. Only the Americans, the Japanese and the Canadians in the hotel were really stuck.

Once I'd eaten and the nice waitress-girl had brought me another coffee, I pulled out the ring from my bag to examine it more closely. It was a signet ring of some kind which was good news for all amateur sleuths trying to ascertain ownership.

But the bad news was that the letters were melted together from the hot caramel. The first letter might be a B or an A or even possibly an F. It was either a man's pinkie ring or a woman's third-finger ring.

I sighed and turned to the other way more important discovery of the night.

The check signed by Barry Simpson.

This was damning any way you looked at it. Add it to his scratched face, and I was sure we had a new contender for prime suspect.

I tapped my fingers on the table and was trying to think what my next step might be when it was pretty much decided for me.

Barry Simpson walked into the breakfast room. Alone.

Immediately, I followed him to the table by the window where he sat down.

"Morning, Barry," I said cheerfully.

He looked up at me and his expression was instantly guarded.

"What do you want?" he said sullenly, staring at my breasts.

Perve. You going down for this is almost as satisfying as Fritz going down for it.

"I was just wondering how you got the scratch," I said.

"I already told you—"

"Yeah, I know you were attacked by a rose bush."

I held up the check I found in the bakery last night. "I think this tells a different story."

As soon as I saw the look on his face—angry and desperate and terrified all at once—it occurred to me that perhaps confronting him without a witness wasn't the wisest course of action. Perhaps I should have gone to the nice Aix police department who had been so open and welcoming every other time I'd approached them.

Not.

"Where did you...?" His eyes were riveted on the check I held in my hand. I took a step back in case he was thinking of snatching it from me.

"Look, I admit I did a bad thing," he said, licking his lips and still staring at the check.

"Is that what investment bankers are calling murder these days?"

"What? No! Not that! I didn't kill Madame Ducharme, I swear it!"

"So what bad thing are you confessing to exactly?"

"I had a fling with Nicole Ducharme."

"You have got to be kidding me," I blurted out.

See? This is how I know I'm a terrible investigator. I cannot for the life of me stop throwing in my value judgment on stuff which I'm sure then considerably slows the momentum of the interrogation. Or stops it dead.

But honestly! Fat old Barry? With *Nicole*? Sometimes I truly do not understand people.

"Nicole's mother was in the back room," Barry said, now looking over my shoulder as if afraid his wife would walk in any minute. "The shop was closed. But the light was on. Nicole mentioned her mother often worked in the back kitchen into the wee hours."

I sat down at his table and the waitress brought us both coffees. At this rate I was heading for a caffeine-induced grand mal seizure.

We waited until the waitress withdrew.

"So you went to pay her a visit why?" I asked.

Barry rubbed a shaking hand across his face as I slipped the check back in my purse.

"I'd tried to talk to Madame Ducharme on several other occasions but she wouldn't talk to me."

"My question still stands."

"Nicole was pregnant," he said bluntly. "She said she would tell my wife about us."

I frowned. All of this just felt so...false. That Nicole would sleep with Barry in the first place was ridiculous. And then she got pregnant?

"What did Nicole hope that would accomplish?"

"I don't know! She wanted me to leave Joanne. At one point, I might have said I would."

"So why were you talking to Madame Ducharme?"

"Because Nicole wouldn't listen to reason! I offered her money for her and the baby to just...let it go, but she came unstrung!"

"Imagine that."

"I thought, since her mother was a businesswoman, she'd take the money and control her daughter."

"But that's not what happened."

"Nicole hadn't told her mother about the baby. When I told Madame Ducharme, she flipped out!" He pointed to his face and the long scratch across his cheek and jaw.

"You gave Madame Ducharme the check?"

"I tried! I must have dropped it. But I swear that woman was alive when I left her."

Remember how I said that Barry was a crap liar? And that the fact that he was lying was written all over his face and showed up like a neon sign pulsing on every lying word he uttered?

Well, he sounded like he was telling the truth about this.

And I didn't think he could have changed so quickly from being a terrible liar to a masterful one. As a result, I could only reach one very unfortunate conclusion.

He was telling the truth.

"What are you going to do with that check?" Barry said, eyeing my purse. "I can pay you twice that amount if you give it back to me and say nothing to anyone."

"What about Elliott? They're holding him for Madame Ducharme's murder."

"Well, maybe he killed her! Did you ever think of that?"

He had a point, I have to admit. I mean, was it really believable that all this happened on the same night that Madame Ducharme was killed? Was it plausible that Barry came, fought with her and left and then Elliott came, fought with her and left and then after all that, the real murderer came, killed her and left?

That was a whole lot of coming and going.

"Did you see anyone outside when you left the bakery?" I asked.

"No. But it was dark. Look, I will make you rich if you give me that check."

"I don't know, Barry. This check is written on an American bank. I'm thinking your money isn't worth anything any more."

"This situation won't last forever! I'm worth millions back in the States."

"Yeah, well, keep telling yourself that. Oh, crap." Just then I looked up to see three Aix policemen talking to the concierge at the front desk. Monsieur Benet was nodding as he spoke to them.

Right up to the point where he turned and pointed at me.

14

Skin in the Game

At least they weren't taking me downtown.

Yet.

Not wanting Barry to think I was losing the upper hand, I quickly intercepted the cops and let them usher me into one of the hotel's private meeting rooms.

"Madame Hooker," the big ugly detective called Brigadier Sommet said severely, "where were you last night at one o'clock?"

"Ummm, sleeping in my little bed?" I said sweetly.

"Can anyone confirm that?"

"I beg your pardon, Lieutenant, but how dare you ask me such a question?"

Sommet blushed and I saw one of the other cops stifle a grin.

"I am only asking if anyone can vouch for that," Sommet said.

"I am an unmarried woman," I said indignantly. "I do not know how they do things here in France, but where I come from that is a serious allegation against my reputation." I took in a big breath. Was it really possible he was buying this?

"I am sorry, Madame," Sommet said. "We have had a complaint from someone who claims you broke into his establishment last night."

I made a *little-ol'-me?* gesture at my form fitting dress that hit me well above the knees and my kitten sandals as if to promote the absurdity of such a claim.

"Do I *look* like a burglar?" I said sweetly. But my mind was racing. If they had no other proof—and *if* Nicole hadn't seen me—it should be my word against Fritz's and that was all to the good except it meant I couldn't present the evidence I'd found last night—damning evidence that laid suspicion at Barry Simpson's feet and helped to exonerate Elliott—without implicating myself.

The cops exchanged glances.

"You have already been the guest of my department for one night, Madame," Sommet said as if to dispel any notion I might have about him believing my general innocence. "I would ask you to stay away from Ducharme's *pâtisserie* and specifically the Ducharme family."

"Did your so-called witness pick Elliott White out of a lineup?" I said, as they were moving toward the door. "I only ask because there were no streetlights that night and it was dark. And who is this guy anyway? Elliott has the right to face his accuser, you know."

"The witness is not White's accuser," Sommet said with frustration "The state of France is."

"So that's all you have?" I snorted. "There is no way a jury will convict him on so little."

"We have more. The very fact that White is American goes against him."

I knew it! Profiled and condemned because he's American!

"What do you mean?" I asked innocently.

"The body was desecrated in a way no Frenchman could ever have done."

What the heck did that mean? I thought. But it was clear he wasn't going to fill me in.

"The real point," I said, trying to prod him to say more, "is that without real evidence or a confession, you have nothing."

"White has confessed to being at the bakery that night."

"So what? Has he confessed to killing Madame Ducharme?"

"No, but we have only just begun questioning him."

"I have spoken to someone else who was at the bakery that night."

"You are lying."

"I certainly am not!"

"What is his name?"

"How do you know it's a him?"

"I do not have time for these games."

I don't know why I was hesitating to give them Barry's name. But something made me feel that if I did they would just swap one American for another. And besides I had no proof—beyond the check which really could be totally unrelated to the murder just as Barry said it was.

And of course, if I tried to show them the check now, they'd ask how I came by it and I'd be back in the slammer. What a conundrum!

"I heard there was a dog barking in the alley," I said. "Was it the same as the dog walker witness? Are Nicole and her father ruled out as suspects? What about Agnes Valentin? Have you finished interviewing *all* the Americans connected to Elliott?"

"We have our suspect. You will stop meddling in police business immediately. This is a warning."

"What about the competing bakeries?" I said, walking with him as he and his men exited the hotel. "Albert Bliss certainly stood to gain by Madame Ducharme's death."

Sommet visibly squirmed, which made me think he hadn't questioned Bliss.

"So did half the bakers in Aix," Sommet said defensively.

Yeah, except none of them were rooting around in the victim's recipe drawer the day after the murder.

"A *real* murder investigation—like one done in the US," I said, going for blood, "would question every one of the bakers in town, no matter how long it took."

That one hit nerves I'm sure Brigadier Sommet didn't even know he had. While he was busy turning purple and groping for his next invective, I went in for the kill.

"You didn't even question Bliss, did you?"

"Monsieur Bliss was not in Aix at the time," Sommet said.

His answer took the air out of my tires just a bit I can tell you. While I was regrouping for another attack, he shoved a very large finger in my face, his fury pinging off him like boinking radar beeps.

"If I hear of you anywhere near Béchmels again I will lock you up for the rest of the year," he said, baring his teeth at me.

Civil liberties much?

"Hey, suits me," I said with a carefree toss of my hair as the three men strode away. "I haven't eaten so good in weeks."

Sommet turned to glare at me. "Remind me to give you the American menu," he said. "It's not nearly as nice."

❀ ❀ ❀ ❀ ❀

The visit from the cops must have taken more out of me than I realized because I spent the rest of the morning lying low and being tortured by my thoughts.

The memory of the snugness of my size four slacks yesterday had me rethink my plans to run out for a *jambon sandwich* at lunchtime and instead I stayed in my room alternately trying to sort out whether Barry really could be the killer and what I'd need to do in order to pin it on Fritz.

I have to say it was immensely annoying to risk life and limb last night and not find anything incriminating on Monsieur Ducharme.

Brigadier Sommet had said that the way the body was had been desecrated.

Good God! What in the world had happened to the poor woman?

I pulled out the signet ring and set it on the dresser before showering and shampooing my hair again and attempting to do something with it before finally succumbing to pinning it up in a loose Gibson Girl. It looked very sexy, I have to say. Not that there was anyone to appreciate it.

Just as those words formed in my head there was a knock on the door. Hating myself for hoping it might be Luc, I opened the door to find Jim standing there.

"Hey," he said. "You look great."

"Thanks," I said, feeling immediately embarrassed. We'd had a decent evening together but honestly it had begun to go down hill after Luc showed up. My heart just wasn't in it after that and I probably telegraphed the fact.

I'd never really gotten any sort of subtle messages from Jim that he'd hoped the *apéro* might turn into dinner which would then turn into bed, but since my base assumption is that that's most men's hope, I figured he might be a little disappointed with me at the moment.

"I'm headed back to Chabanel and was wondering if you wanted to come too."

"You have a car?" I asked in astonishment. Where was he keeping it? Why wasn't he endlessly circling the city like poor Thibault?

"No, it's a bike but I know where I can borrow one for you, too."

"A bike? It's like ten miles to Chabanel, isn't it?"

"Something like that."

Did he really think I was that kind of girl? The athletic, outdoorsy type? *Boy, he really hasn't been listening, has he?*

"I'm still very involved in my investigation," I said, "but if you could swing by and see *les soeurs* when you get back to Chabanel, I'd appreciate it."

"Investigation?" he frowned. "I thought that was finished."

I could feel the first wave of annoyance ripple through me. Jim knew perfectly well it wasn't finished. Elliott was still being held for murder and I still had no real leads.

Jim was clearly just one more man in a long line of men who refused to take me seriously. I hated to see this tendency in him. It wasn't a deal breaker. Honestly, how could it be? I'd have to give up on all men forever if it was. But it was still disappointing.

"Nope," I said. "But thanks for the bike ride offer and please tell the twins I'll be back as soon as I can."

"What for?" Jim asked bluntly, obviously annoyed that I wasn't running around with gleeful anticipation of a spandex biking excursion over the back roads of rural France. "I thought you didn't have an apartment there anymore."

See this is the thing about guys who think they've been shot down. They get cranky. I liked Jim and I didn't want to see him like this. I wanted him to walk away, take a breath, and go back to being the nice guy I knew he basically was. It was up to me to make sure he didn't say something now that was going to royally piss me off.

"Well, we'll see, I guess," I said pleasantly. "I need to run right now, though. Thanks again for the offer and let me know when you're back in Aix."

I should have kissed his cheek but that was more playacting than I was in the mood for. Frankly, it was all I could do to keep the smile on my face as I closed the door.

As soon as I heard his footsteps walking away down the hall, I turned back to the ring on the dresser and did my best to push Jim's expectations and disappointments from my mind. I wanted him as a friend at the very least and did not intend to allow his bruised male ego to hurt the prospect of that.

I picked up the ring. Was that first letter an A? It was a heavy ring which made me think it must have belonged to a man but I once knew a girl in college who wore her beau's school ring on her and it weighed the same as a boat anchor.

But how could I run any kind of scenario in my head of *how* Madame Ducharme was killed—which hopefully involved a vat of caramel—if I didn't know the basic facts of how she was killed?

I put the ring back in my purse next to Barry's check and went to add a little more blush to my cheeks. Maybe I would pop out just for a quick beignet or almond croissant. Maybe if I just ate half instead of the whole thing?

Another knock came on the door, lighter than Jim's had been.

When I went to answer it I was so surprised to see who it was that I just stood there for a moment with my mouth open.

Nicole Ducharme pushed past me and looked around the room.

Immediately my mind beginning to vibrate with one question after another about the possible reasons for her visit.

"I thought you should know that we are posting a guard at the bakery. If you try to break in again, you will be caught. The police have assured us that you will be detained indefinitely."

"Thanks for the heads up."

Nicole bit her lip and rubbed her hands together.

"Is that all?" I asked.

"I need to ask you to return to me anything you...found last night."

I hesitated. She couldn't possibly have known about the ring or she'd have retrieved it herself. Right? So what does she think I found?

I decided to stall to see if she'd tip her hand.

"I can imagine how badly you'd want it back," I said, hoping she'd fill in the blanks.

"So you admit you took it?"

"I'll tell you what I know if you tell me what you know."

I could see she wanted to argue with me or better yet, threaten me, but something—*self-preservation perhaps?*—prevented her.

"*D'accord*," she said biting the word out between her teeth. "What do you want to know?"

"How did your mother die?"

She frowned as if unsure that this very basic question could really be so important to me.

"The doctor said blunt force trauma."

"Which tells me nothing," I said, determined I was not going to be deterred this time.

"*Maman* was...she was hit on the head. She died immediately."

"Did they find the murder weapon?"

Nicole grimaced. "*Oui*. It was the caramel paddle."

"I don't know what that is."

Nicole spoke slowly as if speaking to an idiot. "*Maman* was killed with the caramel churning paddle."

The ring! The murderer lost his or her ring when he or she grabbed for the paddle! Omigosh I have a real honest-to-God clue!

Suddenly a wave of consternation came over me. If Nicole doesn't know about the ring, then what did she come here to get returned?

"Now it is my turn," Nicole said.

"Not yet. What did Brigadier Sommet mean by the body was *desecrated*?"

Nicole winced and walked over to my window. At first I wasn't sure she was going to answer. Finally she turned and said, "*Maman*'s killer arranged her on the floor. He...he threw cherries over her and dumped a canister of flour on top of her."

Weird. What the heck did that mean?

Nicole stretched out her hand.

"And now the check. I know you found it. I'd hidden it on the custard bowls shelves and it wasn't there."

I forced myself not to glance at my purse where the check was. Even if I was afraid to show it to the cops, it was still evidence and might eventually help free Elliott. I couldn't give it up.

"The check was written out to your mother, not you," I said, confirming that I did indeed have it.

Her hand formed a fist and her face flushed with exasperation. "That money was intended for me," she said hotly.

"Why don't you just get Barry to write you another one? I'm sure he would."

Her back stiffened and she didn't answer me, telling me that the money was not the point about the check for her. I decided to go fishing.

"How is it Barry gave your mother the check the night she died," I asked, "and *you* were somehow able to retrieve it and hide it on the shelf?"

"I saw it after finding her body. I had to hide it before the police came. Before..."

"Before your father found it?"

Two tears rolled down her cheeks.

Crap. This was starting to sound like Fritz didn't do it. And that was exceedingly annoying.

"Papa cannot find out," Nicole said, her eyes probing mine beseechingly.

"Which part? About Barry Simpson or about the baby?"

Nicole's shoulders sagged and she dropped to a sitting position on my bed. "Both. If Papa finds out he will kill me," she said.

"You mean *kill you*—like he killed your mother?"

"Don't be absurd. Papa did not kill my mother. The American boy White killed her." She forcefully composing herself and held out her hand again. "The check. Please."

"I'd give it to you, Nicole, but it won't do you any good. You can't cash it."

Her face fell. "Did you already give it to the police?"

"No, but I intend to. Barry admitted he was there that night in your bakery *and* that he fought with your mother. He has more motive for the murder than Elliott does."

"Please! I need to ask you not to involve Monsieur Simpson."

"He's pretty involved all on his own. I'm sorry, Nicole. But if you're afraid of your father hurting you when he learns the truth, you should go to the police."

She straightened her shoulders and walked to the door. I know I had nothing to give her in exchange but I did have one more very important question that I'd hope she'd answer for me.

"Nicole, can I ask you if your father owns a signet ring?"

Nicole paused, her back to me before pulling open the door and stepping into the hall.

"*Non*," she said, quietly. "Papa does not wear jewelry."

So that was another dead end. I followed Nicole out to the hall. She was such a strange young woman. Not particularly sad about her mother's murder, afraid about what her dirt-bag of a father thinks of her, and perfectly capable of sleeping with Barry Simpson...a very strange girl.

"Except," Nicole said, turning back to me as if just remembering something. "I do know someone who wears a signet ring."

I felt a tingling all the way down to my toes.

"Who?" I asked, my heart beginning to pound in anticipation.

"Agnes Valentin."

15

Sweetening the Pot

Luc sat at a café table with Colbert and Dubois. The weather was fine—as it usually was for midday in August. Both the men sitting at the table with him had seen dramatic losses in their inventories. Neither was completely sure it wasn't because of the other one looting their stocks.

Etienne Colbert raised and butchered pigs. Jean Dubois grew strawberries.

While they didn't appear to the casual observer to be competitors, Luc guessed that something else was going on. He'd heard a rumor that Colbert's daughter was seeing Dubois, a man old enough to be her father.

Whatever was going on between the two men Luc did not have the manpower to deal with it. But he knew if either Colbert or Dubois continued to "handle" the situation by attacking each other's livelihoods, there would soon be bloodshed.

"How much is missing?" Luc asked, not bothering to write it down because he wanted to give the impression that this was all informal and a strictly unofficial police matter.

"This week I have lost almost a thousand kilos," Dubois said.

"Impossible!" Colbert responded. "Nowhere near that!"

The two men glared at each other.

"I see this method that the two of you have devised is not helping your situation," Luc said dryly. "But neither is bringing the police into it unless you want to risk deportation."

The rumors had been circulating that the police would soon be resorting to banishment to handle the overflow of lawbreakers. As bad as a few weeks in the village jail might be, being sent away would be nothing short of catastrophic. And while the rumors at this point were just rumors, Luc knew when to use that sort of thing to his advantage.

"So it's true?" Dubois said. "The police are banishing people now?"

Luc shrugged, using that time-classic Gallic shrug that could mean yes or no or anything in between.

"If I find a culprit—for *anything*, be it theft or battery—I cannot process them as in the old days. You see this, yes?"

Both men nodded solemnly.

Luc signaled to the waiter for his bill and the two men took the gesture for what it was—a dismissal. They thanked him, eyed each other and left the café together heading in the direction of the Bar à GoGo.

They were both good men. Luc very much hoped they would be able to work out something between them. The owner of the café set Luc's bill down. Luc knew it would be for much less than it should be and he had long since stopped arguing with the owner about it.

"It was wonderful as usual, Romain," he said as he laid a few euros on the bill.

As he took a last sip of his coffee before heading back to work, he saw something that caught his eye and made him stop.

Jim Anderson was striding across the main square toward one of the two village bakeries.

Luc felt a warm flush on the back of his neck.

Had Jules come back? He took a few steps to see past the fringe of plane trees in order to see if Anderson was alone but the big American had already stepped into the *boulangerie*.

If Anderson was back did that mean Jules was back too? And since she no longer had an apartment in Chabanel, where was she staying?

Unless it was with Anderson?

❊ ❊ ❊ ❊ ❊

After Nicole left I sat on my bed and stared at the signet ring.

Now that I was thinking it might belong to Agnes it made all kinds of sense. The melted letter on the front could definitely be an A. In fact, now that I was thinking of it that way, it was all I could see.

Definitely an A.

My next question, of course, was what was the ring doing at the bottom of the caramel vat unless it came off during the struggle that killed Madame Ducharme? Agnes was certainly tall enough to manage it. And she had motive too. Plus, she worked at the bakery so she had access.

On the other hand, what if Agnes didn't own a signet ring at all? What if Nicole was throwing Agnes to the wolves to put me off the scent? To protect her father?

I looked closely at the ring again. The first letter could definitely, possibly, be an F too. Nicole could also definitely be lying about her father not wearing jewelry to protect him.

My head was whirling. I had too many almost-suspects and nothing really jumped out as sure. I slipped the ring and check back into my bag and left my room to walk down the hall.

I knocked on Jane and Glenn White's door. Glenn opened the door and I have to say he did not look happy to see me. In fact, he just mumbled something and pushed past me and hurried down the hall. Thinking that maybe he and Jane had had a fight or he was just upset because of what he and Jane were going through, I chose to believe it meant nothing.

Jane however was a different matter.

"Oh, it's you," she said as I stood in the door. She was standing in the middle of the room with her arms wrapped around her shoulders as if she were cold.

"Hey, Jane," I said, stepping into the room. The bed was unmade and clothes were in a rumpled tangle on the floor. I'm not sure what was going on with these two. Does horror and worry over a child going to prison for murder really translate into such astonishing untidiness?

Or maybe they're just slobs?

I stepped over a suitcase that was upside down, its contents spilled out onto the carpet.

This was either a failure to clean up after a home invasion or these two had had a knock-down drag out and hadn't gotten around to straightening the furniture yet.

"Can I help you?" Jane said tersely.

"Well, it's me that's supposed to be helping you, remember?" I said lightly, trying not to take it personally that she was acting so cold.

"I'm in a hurry," Jane said, picking up her handbag from the bed. "They said they would allow us to talk to Elliott this afternoon."

"That's great," I said, wading further into the pigsty of a room and finding a pen and notepaper on the desk under what looked like Glenn's dirty socks. I jotted down a few questions on the notepad and then ripped it off and handed it to Jane. "If you could get Elliott to answer these few questions for me, I think we may be onto something."

In my experience, any gesture of action at all helps people who are feeling discouraged to feel more optimistic. It gives them hope that something is being done. That wasn't the sole reason I'd written a brief list of questions for Jane to give to Elliott but it was at least in part.

I might as well not have bothered.

Managing not to look me in the eye, she took the list, shoved it in her purse, and left the room with me standing there.

Not *thanks* or *I'll see he gets it* or *have a nice life.*

Nothing.

Something was going on with those two. Something that—along with their hotel room—did not smell at all right.

16

Cookies Officially Crumbling

It was half past five when I left the hotel to walk toward the Cours Mirabeau in search of sustenance. The light was gorgeous this time of day and other people must have thought so too because the famous promenade was crowded with people enjoying the late afternoon.

La Bouche was the nearest *boulangerie* to the hotel and besides, I was about to make a formal if private pronouncement that La Bouche made the best almond croissants on the planet but I needed to do a little more independent research.

It hadn't taken me long to decide that I needed to cut both Jane and Glenn a break. I had no idea of the kind of stress they were both under and I do tend to be a bit of a clean-freak myself. Just because they hadn't picked up the aftermath of their fight was no reason to think there was anything more sinister going on.

That's what I told myself anyway.

As I approached the bakery I saw that Tattoo Guy who'd waited on me before was stacking and rearranging items in the front window. He was carefully placing little golden cakes on a cascading display. Glossy wheels of cinnamon sticks lapped each other in circles created an optical illusion that made you think they were actually rotating.

As I watched his hands skillfully arrange the confectionary, I saw the glitter of a gold ring on his right pinkie finger. He looked up at me and smiled and I mimed that I'd like to talk to him. He pointed to the front door as if to say he'd meet me there.

I walked over to the threshold of the front door to wait. I was very aware that I hadn't interviewed anyone from the competing bakeries in Aix—and I knew for sure that Lieutenant Do-Nothing hadn't done it.

Tattoo Guy's little dog Cocoa was tied up by the front door and yipping impatiently at being left alone.

Must be nice to bring your dog to work, I thought as I reached down to pet her. She licked my hand and began squirming like she wanted to jump up on me but she was too well behaved.

Good thing. These were my favorite twill slacks.

"Cocoa likes you," Tattoo Guy said as he joined us. He handed me a small bag which held a warm almond croissant. I noticed the ring again.

I'd already registered that gold signet rings seemed to be a common piece of jewelry for both men and women in Aix. Did having one rule him out? Had he ever been in the running? Did it mean anything at all?

I thanked him for the croissant and then nodded at Cocoa, "I'm pretty sure she likes most people."

He laughed. "It's true. She's still a puppy and does not know a stranger."

"You must think it very strange my asking to talk with you," I said as he untied the dog and led us across the street to a sidewalk bench. Cocoa settled at his feet to better look adoringly into her master's eyes.

"You are saying it is unusual for a beautiful woman to want to talk with me?" he said with an arched eyebrow.

"I'm sure *that's* not at all unusual," I said with a laugh, blushing at the compliment. "My name is Jules Hooker."

"Raoul Dubbonet," he said. "*Enchanté.*"

"Ditto. Can I ask how long you've worked at La Bouche?"

His eyebrow arched again but this time without any hint of humor.

"A year," he said, watching me carefully.

"And your English is so good," I said, letting the question hang.

"I lived in Orlando for my senior year of high school."

"Oh!" I don't know why but I did not expect that. "Wow. Really?"

"I worked in the French section of Epcot Center in the summer at Disney World. I was very authentic at the French restaurant there."

I laughed. "I'll bet you were. Did you like the States?"

"Very much. But my student visa expired." He shrugged.

We sat quietly for a moment while I framed my next question.

"I was wondering if you'd heard about the murder at Ducharme's?"

Honestly, without a newspaper or radio, I wouldn't be at all surprised to hear he didn't know about it.

"Only that Madame Ducharme was murdered in her own vat of caramel and doused with flour."

Okay. So he knew more than I had until this morning. Guess the Aix gossip mill must be finer tuned than I'd realized.

"I guess La Bouche must be happy to see Ducharme's closed," I said.

He cocked his head at me and frowned. "You mean because of the competition?"

"It's just that I noticed that La Bouche has done a ton of business ever since Ducharmes closed its doors."

He leaned down to tousle Cocoa's ears.

"I suppose," he said finally. "But I do not think Monsieur Bliss cares."

"Really? He doesn't care that his bakery is benefiting from Madame Ducharme's death?"

"They were friends. I'm sure Monsieur Bliss finds no joy at how La Bouche is benefiting from her death."

"Are you sure? Because that would be unusual if it's true."

"Monsieur Bliss inherited a lot of money last year. Already he is planning on opening a new, bigger bakery in Nice."

There goes the professional motive, I thought with a sigh.

"And the rest of the bakeries in Aix aren't anywhere in Ducharme's league," Raoul said. "It would be like 7-11 trying to compete with Wal-Mart, you know?"

I nodded begrudgingly. Thinking of one of the competing bakeries as being involved in the murder had always been a long shot. The murder felt way too personal for that.

"Sorry for the third degree," I said, feeding a piece of my croissant to Cocoa who happily scarfed it down. "I'm trying to find reasons why the man the police think killed Madame Ducharme is innocent."

"The American boy? I am sorry if I have not helped."

"Oh, you have, Raoul. Thank you. And thank you for the croissants. They're the best in Aix."

"*Mais non!* In all of France!" He grinned and I saw his passion and delight in talking about pastries and wondered if he'd had a hand in making the croissants I loved so much.

After I left Raoul and Cocoa, I made my way back to the Cours Mirabeau. My intention was to find a private little table to watch the light fade into another perfect south of France evening and try to put my thoughts together over what I'd learned today.

I figured I had just enough euros left for one or possibly two *Kir Royales*.

As I watched the light fade, I thought of Raoul and what he must have thought of Disney World and his American high school and how that must have affected him. He was very cute and I guessed he was about my age but I got the definite impression he was more interested in my reaction to his croissants than in me.

The French and their food—they take it all very seriously, make no mistake.

Just as I signaled for my second drink and was beginning to settle into some serious rumination about Luc and where he fit into my worldview about now, I reached for my bag to make sure I had enough money.

Which was when I discovered that my bag—with the ring and check in it—was gone.

17

Deeply, Darkly, Desperately

I got on my hands and knees and groped the dirty sidewalk, knocking aside cigarette butts and worse in the hopes that my bag had just fallen off the back of my chair and gotten kicked aside.

No such luck.

Sickened, I stood up and looked at the people sitting in the café with me. I'd paid them no mind when I first came in but now they were all looking at me as I brushed off my slacks and glared at them accusingly.

Someone had stolen my bag.

Someone had inched up behind me as I stared moonily out at the grand boulevard—unmindful of my surroundings—and lifted my bag.

My favorite Kate Spade bag with the only two pieces of evidence that might help Elliott White go free.

I felt nauseated.

Was I being followed? Or was this just a random snatch and grab?

The waiter came to me with my drink and I waved him away, pointing to the few coins I had on the table that would cover the first drink. He didn't care. He'd probably guzzle my drink on the way back to the bar. *Tant pis* clueless American tourist!

I was so angry with myself. What's the point of breaking into a place at night that's guarded by a certifiable maniac if you're not going to keep an eye on the prizes you found from that excursion?

I walked back to the hotel with no flashlight and no wallet—my favorite lip gloss gone—and once more back to square one on the case. As I walked I noticed movement above me. The light was just enough to see several cats running along the rooftops. Feral, for sure. I wondered how they survived.

I winced as I pulled open the door to the Hotel Cezanne and hoped that Luc would do what he said and make sure Neige was okay.

Monsieur Benet was at the front desk and waved to me when he saw me enter.

"A message for you, Madame Hooker," he said. "Delivered by a very scary individual indeed, *non*?"

I took the envelope from him and recognized the handwriting as one of the Madame Twins. Thibault no doubt was the very scary mailman that Monsieur Benet was referring to.

I asked for another room key, thanked him and began the long trudge up to the third floor and my respite from the world. As I did I couldn't help rerun the list of suspects in my head.

There was Fritz—wife beater and my first pick as the murderer. Then Nicole—she had opportunity and didn't seem to love her mother but generally looked weak on motive. As for Agnes—possibly the owner of the signet ring—she hated Madame Ducharme for firing her and taking her away from Nicole and had no alibi. Barry Simpson apparently had motive out the wazoo, opportunity and means. But he didn't feel right to me for this.

I pushed open the door to my room and saw the two fat candles on the dresser. It was dark inside so I gratefully lit them both.

As I watched the flickering flames my mind kept shuffling and reshuffling through all the possibilities until I came to Albert Bliss, the owner of La Bouche. I couldn't help but think with a name like *Bliss* they'd missed the boat on naming his bakery.

Anyway, Bliss had possibly the weakest motivation of all. I mean, was it really believable—even in France—that someone would murder for a caramel tart recipe?

I sat down on the bed and felt the exhaustion of the day cascade over me.

And then there was Elliott and I was not one hundred percent sure he didn't do it. His parents knew something, that was clear.

I was very much afraid that what they knew was that their son had killed Madame Ducharme.

A splinter of despondency jabbed into me. *That's just perfect*, I thought. *So after losing the only two clues that I'd risked life and limb to procure, it's completely possible that on top of everything I've taken the case of a guilty man.*

And that was my fault because, honestly, had I even cared when I took the case to know if he was guilty?

I'd screwed this up so badly. All of it. I couldn't help feel that I was now in the process of digging myself out of hole. I was so much worse off now—even than when I'd first landed in Provence and realized I was stranded here. At least then I'd had a few friends.

At the thought of *les soeurs*, I felt a shot of pleasure at receiving a letter from them and instantly ripped open the envelope.

It would have been better if I'd lost it by falling down the stairwell.

My French is bad but even I could understand the gist of the note.

Don't come back. We don't want you. You let us down. Typical American.

I sat in my half-darkened room, the terrible letter in my hands and did what any self-respecting private eye would do when her case was coming apart—I burst into tears.

How could things get any worse? Luc thinks I'm with Jim—who think's I'm not to be taken seriously—and the Madame Twins want me out of their lives.

I have not *one* shred of evidence to help poor Jane and Glenn White with their current nightmare—except possibly to make it worse by saying I've uncovered some evidence that supports that Elliott might have killed Madame Ducharme.

And as for the few people I'd connected with in Aix —Joanne and Barry both hate me and are actively avoiding me and the only other person who used to like me is some dude with tats who gave me free croissants and who I left a few hours ago not being able to get rid of me fast enough.

Could things get any worse?

And dear God, when will I quit asking that?

Because just at that moment, I heard loud voices in the hall. I jumped off the bed and ran to my door and swung it open.

Jane White was there, standing with her arms crossed and looking down at her feet. She was listening to the commotion downstairs. At least two or three people were talking agitatedly below. Jane glanced at me and shook her head.

"Poor Monsieur Benet," she said. "They've just found little Beignet run over in the alley behind the train station."

My gut wrenched at her words. She turned to me, her face impassive but still refusing to look me in the eye as she shoved a scrap of paper in my hands.

"For all the good it'll do," she said as she walked back to her room. When she shut the door to her room Joanne was suddenly visible where she was standing in the doorway of her room. She looked at me.

"Here's hoping you do a better job with Elliott than you did for poor Monsieur Benet's dog," she said acidly.

❀❀❀❀❀

I had to get out of there.

I was grateful that Jane hadn't been present to hear Joanne's comment but even if she hadn't I couldn't stay in that hotel a minute longer.

It was a little past eight in the evening when I scooped up a flashlight from the front desk and slipped out undetected amid all the noise and sadness in the lobby. Monsieur Benet was openly sobbing about his little dog and I can't remember feeling more responsible for something I never had anything to do with in my life.

I headed toward the center of the old part of Aix. The last thing I wanted to see was a bustling café and re-live the fact that I'd lost my only two clues in one this afternoon.

But it wasn't until I was nearly to the Aix cathedral that I realized where I'd been unconsciously heading ever since I'd bolted out of the Hotel Cezanne.

I was in the student ghetto just around the corner from Agnes Valentin's apartment.

Thinking of Agnes made me think of the note that Jane had shoved into my hands. I found an empty stone bench and sat down.

It was Elliott's answers to my questions. In answer to my question *Do you own a signet ring?* Jane had written in a shaky hand *No.*

Did Agnes own one? Yes.

My pulse began to race. *So it's true! Agnes has a signet ring!* A ring with the first letter A!

I scanned the next few lines.

Did you hear anything when you left the bakery that night? No.

Did you see anyone in the alley when you left? No.

At the bottom of the note was a sentence inside a brace of parenthesis and obviously written hurriedly. Frowning, I tried to make out Jane's cramped handwriting. Finally I deciphered it and my heart fell when I did.

It read, *E said he gave the ring to Agnes and she gave it back to him when they broke up last week.*

My shoulders sagged and I felt a distinct heaviness in my core as yet another clue pointed to Elliott's guilt.

This is bad, I thought. The one clue that I had that did NOT point to Elliott up until now had been the stupid ring. If Agnes confirmed this to the police, Elliott might as well start his march to the *guillotine* right now.

Is that why the White's were acting so weird? Is it because they know their son killed Madame Ducharme and they're praying I'll find enough doubt to keep him from hanging?

Because the Whites were definitely acting weird.

I glanced down the street where Agnes Valentin's apartment building was. Might as well hear what she has to say. Might as well hear from her own lips if she intends to throw Elliott under the bus.

Mind you, I no longer had the ring. I'd lost the one thing that would put the final nail in Elliott's coffin. That's good news in a way. Except whoever took it from me now has that power.

Perhaps it didn't matter? But I knew it did. Even without the ring to prove it one way or the other I needed to find out the truth.

As I walked to Agnes's apartment building I couldn't help but realize that every time I made an attempt to find a clue or dig a little deeper I found something that implicated Elliott.

Maybe Jim is right, I thought. Maybe I should find another way to make a living.

Even though he hadn't come right out and said it, I'd read it plain enough in his face. He'd done everything but roll his eyes every time I talked about *my case*.

I rang the bell on the apartment building and as before was immediately buzzed in. I went up the curving flights of stairs and knocked on Agnes's door. It popped open as soon as I touched it and I could smell the rank, fading aroma of weed emanating from within.

"*Bonjour?*" I called, stepping inside. "Hello, Agnes? Are you here?"

This is how I know I'm cut out for this business because as soon as I had an opportunity to snoop around someone's apartment I didn't think twice. I didn't say *oops* and close the door. I didn't wait outside calling her name.

I went for it. Without hesitation. I recognized a lucky break when I saw it and in seconds I was across the foyer and into the living room of Agnes' apartment.

All the while my mind was coming up with perfectly believable excuses to give if Agnes came out of the bathroom with a towel wrapped around her head wondering what I was doing in her apartment.

Agnes's place was a very typical dormitory style affair for a single student which in itself I thought unusual. She was a student working her way through her studies. How could she afford her own place without a roommate? It wasn't a palace but it was decent.

You know how people say they have a sixth sense about something that was about to happen?

Well, I can officially say that I am *not* one of those people.

Because I had no inkling as to what I'd find as I crept through the quiet rooms. There was absolutely no psychic tip off in any way.

No hint that when I turned the corner into the kitchen I would find Agnes sitting in one of the bistro chairs, her head cocked to one angle, her eyes glassy and staring blankly at me.

18

Sweet Surrender

Don't judge me.

I saw she was dead and I just stood there, my mind racing. Well, it was really more like pinging and bouncing action, than racing. Like a pinball banging off the spasmodic flippers in my head.

Being the observant type as well as a trained investigator I could see straight off that she was dead. Plus, the unnatural twist of her head, the staring dead eyes and the big purple bruises on her throat pretty much laid it out for me.

I stood in the kitchen staring at her for at least a full minute until my ping-ponging thoughts could settle into some kind of plan of action. I'm not proud of the fact that my first thought was to get the hell out of here.

And not because I thought the killer might still be lurking about—*which I totally should have been thinking* —but because I knew the person who finds the body is always the prime suspect.

And I had enough on my plate without being arrested for murder.

I listened for any noises in the apartment and the hallway. I took a step closer to the body, knowing I needed to get out as soon as I could, but also knowing this was my only chance to examine the crime scene.

I noticed she was not wearing any jewelry and that there were two wine glasses on the table. It was only now just nine o'clock. So unless she'd *just* been killed—which wasn't likely since the cheese on the plate in front of her had already crusted over—this happened last night. With someone she considered a friend or at least a congenial drinking buddy.

No lipstick on either glass. But then Agnes was a student. It'd be a miracle if she were wearing undergarments, let alone lipstick.

There was nothing else was on the table. I scanned the counter and saw a small bag of tomatoes and a croissant on a dish. Feeling reasonably sure the cops didn't have fingerprint kits and even if they did they didn't have *mine* on file, I opened the fridge.

Typical student. A bottle of white wine. A lemon. And a takeout bag.

I felt the perspiration form on my top lip. Noises in the hallway alerted me to activity out there.

Had I closed the front door behind me? I was almost positive I hadn't.

Just as I turned to go, I spotted the cabinet under the sink and on impulse pulled it open. The trash can was there. Inside I saw a wine bottle cork. And a small bag with the logo of La Bouche on it.

I stared at the pastry bag. La Bouche was nowhere near Agnes's apartment. But if, like me, she had a thing for their almond croissants it's possible she'd make the trek.

There were more voices in the hall now. I hurried back across the foyer feeling a deepening sadness catch me in the throat.

Agnes had been snotty and alive just a few hours ago, her whole life ahead of her.

If her death had anything to do with Madame Ducharme's murder—*and how could it not?*—then Elliott was off the hook.

I hesitated in the apartment foyer and waited until the voices faded. Then I stepped out into the empty hallway and ran down the stairs.

❄ ❄ ❄ ❄ ❄

He watched the American woman emerge from Agnes' apartment. He watched her stand in front of the building as if uncertain what to do and then she walked to the café across from the building.

What was she doing?

Why was she here?

He cursed in silent frustration.

She would not quit. And now the police were asking more questions! Already they had asked him to come in a second time for *routine* questioning.

No, he had waited too long already. It must be tonight.

Tonight as she walked alone and in the dark.

Tonight he would stop her once and for all.

Tonight he would let the dead answer her questions.

19

Double Whammy

I hated not to report Agnes's murder but honestly even if I wanted to, how could I call it in without a phone? Without implicating myself?

Once I was safely out of her apartment building I went to a café across the street and ordered a water. I felt grateful that the waiter didn't dump it on my head when he brought it to me but I was officially broke and it was either that or do a drink and dash and frankly I didn't have the energy for that even if I'd had the nerve.

I sat in the café until my hands stopped trembling. At one point I thought about throwing a rock into Agnes's window from the alley. Surely someone would report that? But they might also report the sight of me doing it too and let's face it, I am nothing if not memorable.

At least I'd left Agnes' door open. With any luck someone would find her soon and report it and then whatever the Aix cops needed to do they could begin doing it.

La Place des Martyrs de Résistance was catty-corner across the little cobblestone square.

Envisioning the dozen or so young people that had been rounded up by the Gestapo sixty years earlier and hung in this very square where people were now enjoying their *apéros* and olives—and knowing that Agnes had now joined them—just made me want to cry.

What a mess I've made of everything, I thought. No friends, no money, no place to live. No idea if my best friend CeCe in Atlanta is alive or dead—or my mother for that matter.

I allowed the sadness to drift through me. What the hell am I even doing over here? Shouldn't I try to find my way to Paris where the American Embassy is? Surely they know a way for Americans to get back home.

Isn't that what I want? To get back home?

Across from the place where the poor Resistance fighters had met their end a candy shop was still open, the line winding out the door of people who clearly couldn't go a full night without eating something chocolate first.

I watched the people in line, their faces glowing with anticipation, and even counted the number of dogs many of them had with them. Inside, I could see a bigger dog on a leash sniffing at the shelves of candy.

Maybe I should get a dog?

Except I'd probably just kill it.

Suddenly, I heard a scream and when I looked up a young woman was emerging from Agnes's building, her eyes wide with fright and horror.

"Police! Police!" she screamed as passersby surrounded her.

I finished my water and left my table, glad the waiter was distracted enough not to give me a dirty look for leaving without paying or tipping.

I walked away slowly, my head down in defeat and deepening sadness.

Goodnight, Agnes. I'm so sorry I couldn't help you either.

❊❊❊❊❊

Luc was parking his police vehicle two streets away from Jules' hotel and affixing the boot to its right front wheel when he saw her.

It had only taken the briefest of casual conversations with Jim Anderson at the *boulangerie* this afternoon to ascertain that Anderson and Jules were *not* together.

For some reason beyond Luc's normally highly tuned abilities to construe or decipher, that had bizarrely translated into a strong urge to drive to Aix.

Now he watched Jules walk down the dark street as if she were drunk or at the very least in a mental fog of some kind. What was she doing out at this time of evening, alone, and not paying a bit of attention to where she was or who might be around her?

"Jules!" he called out.

She turned and instantly crossed her arms as if to protect herself, belatedly realizing she might be in a vulnerable position.

"Yes?" she called out shakily. "Who is it?"

Luc went to her and saw with gratification as her face burst into a visage of pleasure and relief at the sight of him.

"*C'est moi*," he said as he reached her and leaned in to kiss her cheek.

Instantly, she clung to him and he pulled her close and held her. He could feel her trembling.

"*Qu'est-ce que c'est?*" he said, his naturally protective nature activated on high alert. "What has happened?"

She shook her head. "I'm so glad to see you, Luc. I thought you got the wrong idea and I didn't know how to contact you and I'm just so sorry."

"Shhhh, it is fine now, *chérie*," he said, leading her away from the hotel and back toward the Cours Mirabeau.

If he knew anything, he knew she needed a drink and something to eat.

"The Madame Twins hate me," Jules said, wiping tears from her eyes. "They wrote me this horrid note saying *go to hell* and don't come back and I know they're right. I left so what were they to think?"

Luc wasn't sure Jules wasn't on the verge of hysteria. He'd never seen her so distraught and he'd seen her after she'd discovered a dead body and right after she'd been attacked by two killers.

Tonight was a new one for the books, as the Americans say.

He held her with one arm around her shoulders until they came to the first café and he ordered drinks and dinner for both of them. Once the waiter left, Luc picked up her hand and said kindly but firmly.

"Now, tell me what happened."

First, *les soeurs*. Yes, it sounded as if they were angry with Jules and Luc wasn't surprised. Madame Cazaly especially had latched onto Jules pretty firmly and would be doing her best to protect herself and her sister from any hurt or disappointment from that corner.

"I am sure Madame Cazaly only wanted you to feel guilt-free about going to live your life in Aix," he assured Jules. But she didn't look assured.

"Aix sucks!" she said. "I miss everyone back in Chabanel."

He nodded, trying to tamp down the pleasure at her words. He knew she was just being emotional. "What else?" he asked.

"I found two clues that might help Elliott White," Jules said. She'd stopped sniffling and seemed to be doing much better, especially when the waiter set a plate of steaming *moules frites* in front of her along with a large balloon glass of Pinot Noir. "Only I lost them."

"What clues, *chérie?" And exactly when had he started calling her that?*

"A signet ring that I found in the trap of the caramel vat at the Ducharme's," Jules said, closing her eyes to enjoy a mouthful of buttery, salty *pommes frites* that had come with the mussels. "And a check written by one of the Americans staying at my hotel to Madame Ducharme on the day of the murder."

Luc blinked and took a moment to gather his thoughts before speaking. Jules didn't appear to notice as she was too busy eating. It looked as if she hadn't eaten in a while. He didn't know what to ask her first: how had she gotten these clues or when had she eaten last?

"You are not eating regularly?" he asked frowning.

"I'm eating almond croissants," she said. "But I ran out of money. And then my purse was stolen today."

Mon Dieu! She must of course return with him to Chabanel this very night. This whole idea had been madness from the start. What had any of them been thinking? He felt his anger begin to grow at the thought of Mayor Beaufait insisting that Jules relocate to Aix.

But Jules was quickly finishing her plate and washing it down with the Pinot while she'd been talking.

"*Oui, chérie?*" he said. "What is that you said?"

"I found a dead body tonight."

"My English is not being very good. It sounded like you said—"

"Agnes Valentin was murdered tonight. I went to her apartment to talk to her and found her dead."

Luc stared at Jules, speechless.

"Luc?"

"How?"

"Well, she looked as if she'd been strangled. Her neck was bent."

"*Non,* I mean how...how is it that you found her?"

147

"I told you. I went to talk to her."

"I do not understand." He struggled to realize that not only had Jules found *another* body—but they were half way through their main course before she'd mentioned it to him!

"You found a dead body?" he sputtered.

"This is taking you way longer to understand than usual, Luc," Jules said, tearing off a piece of bread from the *baguette* on the table. "I'm sure she was murdered by the same guy who killed Madame Ducharme. Don't you think?"

"You went to the police?" he said, urgently signaling to the waiter to bring them their bill.

"No," Jules said slowly, watching him with narrowed eyes now. "I didn't want to spend the rest of my life answering questions in a twelfth century dungeon. Luc, you can't tell the cops I found her. And besides, they already know about it. Someone found her after I did."

"Did you...touch anything?" Luc ran a hand through his hair as his mind quickly reverted to professional methodologies.

"Of course not. I've seen enough *Law and Order* episodes not to contaminate the crime scene. As if that matters to the Aix police."

Luc shook his head in bewilderment. "I cannot believe you found another body."

"Well, I don't intentionally go looking for them." Jules wiped the garlic wine sauce of her *moules* up with a piece of bread and popped it into her mouth.

"And you say the police know?" he asked rubbing his chin and frowning.

The waiter brought the bill and Luc paid him, his eyes fixed on a far away point and his thoughts scattered as he tried to bring them back in to focus.

"Luc?"

He looked at her. What in the world had she gotten up to in just three short days?

"The Aix police," Jules said, "for whatever reason—incompetence or collusion—are not on the right track with this murder investigation. Can you understand that? Can you be open to believing that?"

He grunted but didn't answer. He knew Sommet to be an ass who'd risen far above his capabilities. But he was not clever enough to cover up or reroute a murder investigation. At least Luc didn't think so.

"Elliott couldn't have killed Agnes," Jules said. "So it has to be someone else." She leaned in close to him. "If I could just get a glance at the case file."

Could she be right? Were the Aix police hiding something? Covering for someone? It wasn't impossible. And now there was a young student dead?

Luc felt a sudden urge of anger and determination.

"I might be able to help with that," he said.

20

A Wing and a Prayer

All I really heard over the joyous bells ringing in my ears and the delight of sitting across from Luc on what had, up to now been the worst night of my life, was that he was willing to help! He was going to get the case file!

So delighted was I about everything Luc was saying—and knowing for certain now that the end was in sight—that I only half heard the rest of what he was saying...something about letting him work the case as long as I just watched or something like that.

Anyway, none of that mattered. Luc was going to help!

Luc paid the waiter—God bless him—and then we hurried off to the Aix Police Municipale. Luc wisely suggested that I wait for him outside and I was so relieved to finally have a partner in all this and not just any partner but sexy, serious, so sympathetic Luc—that I didn't mind at all.

How many people can say they saw the worst day of their life turn into their best?

Anyway, I gave him my meekest, most believable *whatever you say Luc* face and waited outside the police station under one of the new working streetlamps while he went inside. He wasn't gone twenty minutes.

If I didn't know him better I'd say he swiped the case notes off the Lieutenant's desk but in any case, he was back in a flash, his arm once more around my waist and pulling me through the winding back streets of Aix.

Some day I'll need to ask him how he knows his way around Aix so well. He took me immediately to this little hole in the wall brasserie and ordered coffees and brandies.

Oh, it's nice to be dating a man with a steady paycheck during an apocalypse.

Gosh. Is that what we're doing? Please let that be what we're doing.

As soon as Luc ordered the drinks, he opened the case file. Naturally it was all in damn French but he began to lead me through it.

"Madame Ducharme was battered to death by a caramel paddle at approximately midnight on the night of August 24th," he read.

Seriously. Can you even imagine those words being uttered anywhere but France? No other place would even know what a caramel paddle was.

"The body was then desecrated by the placement of twelve candied cherries and approximately a cup of milled flour."

I tapped my finger against the rim of my brandy glass and frowned in concentration.

Not just *dumped* but *placed*. Like the killer had all the time in the world. Well, wouldn't that be the case if he lived there? Like Fritz did?

But were the cherries a message of some kind? And if so, what possible message was the killer hoping to send with *cherries*?

"What's the word in French for cherry?"

"*Cerise.*"

"That's no help. What's the significance of the flour?" I asked. "Is it because it's white? Dumping flour on a woman would make her look white-headed, right? So was he trying to say she's old? Or maybe too white? Is this a race thing?"

"Perhaps flour was the first thing at hand to throw."

Could the cherries and flour really mean nothing?

"I saw Fritz Ducharme physically abusing his wife," I said.

"*Vraiment?*"

"Hell yeah *vraiment*," I said, draining my coffee cup and reaching for my brandy glass. "And since as the surviving spouse he probably benefits from her death, my question is why isn't Fritz Ducharme the cops' main suspect? Is he not American enough?"

"Monsieur White is being held because there's evidence against him, not because he's American," Luc admonished me.

"What about the eyewitness who saw Elliott?" I asked.

"What about him?"

"Who is he? What's his name?"

Luc frowned. "Why do you want to know his name? Do you intend to harass him at his home or place of work?"

"If by *harass* you mean question politely, then yes I intend to harass him."

"*Non.*"

"*Non*, what? *Non* you won't tell me or *non* you don't know his name?"

"The name isn't listed in the file."

"Then how are they going to call on him to testify?"

"I don't believe they are. The name of the witness isn't here because they failed to get it at the time."

"What? Wait a minute. They can't call their witness? How is that possible?"

"It was an oversight. The officer was young."

"Well, can he at least pick him out of a criminal database?"

"He could, if this witness was a known criminal. Unfortunately our criminal database is all online. *Tant pis.*"

Yeah, big time tant pis.

"We are beginning to print them out as in the old days," Luc said. "But it won't help with this."

"What about the dog?" I asked.

"Comment?"

"It might be easier to identify the dog than the guy. See if the interviewing officer mentioned the dog."

Luc read the folder. "A small Labrador-mix. Black."

I drank my brandy down and closed my eyes to feel it burn all the way down. When I opened my eyes, Luc was watching me. My goodness he had full lips.

"So the cops failed to get the name of the witness but they noted the kind of dog it was?" I said, my head beginning to swim just a bit.

Luc shrugged. "The French love their dogs." He closed the file. "Now what?"

The brandy and the lovely meal and the pleasure of Luc's company gave me a warm glow that I did not want to end.

"I'm less worried than I was," I said, "since for all intents and purposes the prosecution witness doesn't exist. But that still doesn't tell us who killed Madame Ducharme. Or Agnes."

I watched Luc light up a cigarette which surprised me but didn't bother me at all. On the contrary it somehow made me feel very Casablanca.

"So do you think they'll be able to successfully prosecute on the flimsy evidence they have?" I asked.

Luc frowned and gestured to the waiter for the check.

"I agree that they do not have enough evidence," he said.

"But?"

"But nowadays anything can happen."

He was referring to the EMP and the fact that new laws were being written, new harsher rules snapping into place.

It would be unwise to count on how things had always been handled *before*.

"It would be better to find the real murderer," he said.

"You're telling me." I yawned in spite of myself. It was only a little after eleven but it had been an eventful day and I was tired.

"I will take you back to the hotel," Luc said, ever the one to take the reins and plot the course. "Tomorrow, you will return to Chabanel with me."

I felt my pulse quicken and I realized that that was exactly what I wanted to do. Even if I had no idea where in Chabanel I would be living.

"What about Elliott White? I promised his parents I'd help prove him innocent."

"We will think about that from Chabanel," he said and until that moment I hadn't thought any words could mean more to me than *Jules-will-you-marry-me*. But the feeling of relief and comfort was so immense, that I nearly kissed him right then and there.

Instead, I let him take my arm and we wove our way out of the small restaurant and into the darkened back streets.

I only had a bare moment to enjoy the fleeting joy of feeling Luc's presence beside me, his hand strong and sure on the small of my back, and the absence of all worry before a rush of wind and shadow descended on me and I felt myself falling, falling onto the cold, hard cobblestones.

21

Howling at the Moon

Luc saw their assailant a millisecond before the man reached them. Luc swiveled Jules over his hip and behind him, leaving his left side unguarded. He deflected the blow intended for Jules with his shoulder and staggered under the force of it, his breath rocketing out of him.

"*Connard*!" the attacker hissed, raising his club up again to finish the job.

Luc blocked the blow again, this time with his forearm, and felt the pain jolt up into his shoulder blades. Barely recoiling from the hit, he caught the man solidly on the jaw with a left hook and put his entire weight into it.

The man staggered backward, dropping the club onto the stones, but remained upright. Pushing off from the stonewall with one hand, their attacker wobbled into a half run down the alley.

Luc turned to Jules on the ground. Her eyes were wide with wonder as she watched their assailant retreat, his footsteps echoing down the ancient city walkway.

"That was Fritz Ducharme!" she gasped as Luc helped her to her feet.

"I am going after him," Luc said, his arm burning where it had connected with the club. "Go back to the hotel. *Maintenent*."

"Luc, no!" Jules said, grabbing his sleeve. "He's *in* with the Aix police! They'll never believe you!"

157

They were wasting precious time. Luc needed to go after Ducharme *now*.

"Go back to the hotel, Jules. Stay under the streetlamps and go straight back. *Attendez-moi.*"

Jules pulled out of his grip and took two steps in the direction that Ducharme had gone.

"Luc, listen to me! The Aix police are going to see this assault as an isolated event and unconnected to the murder. Don't you see? Nobody wants to clear the American and get the right guy."

Luc grabbed her shoulders firmly.

"*Nobody* on the police force wants the wrong man held for this crime," he said firmly, his anger barely held in check. "Now do what I tell you."

He turned her around and gave her a push in the direction of the Cours Mirabeau before taking off after Ducharme.

❊ ❊ ❊ ❊ ❊

I don't know if I was shaking because of the attack or because I'd been so successfully Alpha-maled by one Luc DeBray but I have to say I was definitely weak in the knees.

Forceful kind of guy, that Luc.

Surely an attack on a policeman trumps whatever deal the Aix cops had going with Ducharme?

In spite of the darkness and the late hour, I wasn't feeling a bit nervous as I began to walk back to the hotel. Maybe because the one person who meant me harm was currently on the run.

As I walked through the quiet streets, I found the new facts of the case racing through my mind. The most startling piece was the fact that the cherries had been *arranged* on Madame Ducharme's head instead of just thrown at her. Almost like she was on display. I slowed my pace as the thoughts began to come faster now.

It was a distinction that mattered and although I wasn't sure exactly how or why, I knew it did.

Who displays pastries for effect? Who creates window displays to entice and allure?

I came to the end of the street which stopped at the mossy, cobblestoned square anchored by the Fountain D'Albertas. In the dark it looked like a big corroding champagne glass with weeds growing out of the top.

The Cours Mirabeau was one block past it which would end with Ducharme's *pâtisserie*. Along the way was La Bouche. As soon as I noted that, my pace picked up and so did my thoughts. In fact my mind raced faster and faster as the pieces began to methodically click into place.

Out of the corner of my eye I saw a figure step out of the stone doorway. I froze in the middle of the street and watched as the figure morphed into a middle-aged woman with a small terrier on a leash. The two moved silently toward the fountain where the woman snapped on a flashlight to see where she was going.

And then it hit me.

It's not the eyewitness that we should be focused on.

It's the dog! It all centers around the dog.

Raoul, the window designer at La Bouche has a black lab. The same kind of dog the mysterious witness was walking on the night of the murder. The same kind of dog that Nicole heard barking under her window during the time of the murder.

Is that just a wild coincidence?

Isn't it my job to pay attention to coincidences?

Raoul must walk his dog near La Bouche—*which is also near Ducharmes.*

My mind began to play out the various scenarios.

Why would *Raoul* kill Madame Ducharme?

Maybe they were lovers?

I glanced at my watch. Eleven thirty p.m.

There was only one way to find out.

As I walked toward La Bouche, my excitement ramping up with every step, I reminded myself that seeing Raoul wearing a signet ring had made me cross him off my suspects list.

Either my theory about him was wrong—and he was innocent—or he'd simply replaced the lost ring. The first letter on the ring could easily have been an R instead of an A.

But that didn't sound plausible. How could Raoul have replaced the ring so soon? Was it possible the ring was irrelevant to what happened to Madame Ducharme? Or maybe it was *her* ring? And she'd lost it herself?

Had I really ruled Raoul out because he was wearing a signet ring? What if the ring has nothing to do with the murder? What if it was lost weeks before?

But I knew that didn't make sense. Nobody would lose his or her ring and carry on making caramel turtles or whatever with it just sitting there in the mesh. The ring was important.

And Raoul hadn't lost a ring.

As I turned down rue Madeleine where La Bouche was, I kicked myself for not asking Nicole more questions about her mother.

On the other hand, Nicole was hardly my most reliable witness.

Besides, surely there were hundreds of Labrador-mix dogs in Aix? Even if you narrowed them down to those living in the blocks nearest Ducharme's, any dog walker might easily walk a mile radius on a nightly walk.

I shook myself out of these negative, conflicting and basically unhelpful thoughts.

Cherchez la chien, I told myself determinedly. *Find the dog.*

See how the other pieces fit after that.

La Bouche was closed at this hour of course but I knew there was likely still someone inside. As committed as Raoul had seemed, I was crossing my fingers that I would get lucky tonight.

I went to the front door. There was a lantern light emanating from behind the counter. I knocked on the glass front door.

Immediately I heard the clip-clip-clip of a woman's pumps making their way across the terrazzo tile floor to the front door. A young woman appeared and frowned at me through the glass pane.

"*Fermé!*" she said sternly.

"I need to talk to Raoul," I said through the glass. "Is he here?"

She gave an expression of extreme annoyance and unlocked the door.

"Raoul not be here," she said icily.

Good Lord how do any of these people ever sell a second donut with this kind of crappy customer service?

"Do you have his home address?"

I knew it wasn't likely she'd give it to me even if she understood me but maybe they did things differently here in France. Maybe she thought I was a girlfriend who couldn't find my way to his place two nights in a row. Maybe she'd...?

"*Il est parti*," she said firmly.

"He goes?" I said. "Oh! You mean, he's gone. Do...you...know...his...home...address?" I spoke slowly, hoping that would make up for her lack of English vocabulary.

"No. He go for good," she said closing the door in my face.

22

Far from Shore

Luc called the Aix police and gave his location as he ran. He could see Ducharme ahead of him. The sounds of both their footsteps pounding the pavement grew louder in Luc's brain as he gained on him.

"Halt!" Luc called, wondering why he wasted precious breath to do it.

Ducharme was coming to the Cours Mirabeau and even at nearly midnight, there were people promenading hand in hand, walking their dogs, out enjoying the night air.

It suddenly occurred to Luc that the man might try to take a hostage. He might try to create a diversion by hurting an innocent bystander and forcing Luc to stop to help them.

Luc ran harder, vaguely aware that people were trying to clear out of his way.

Ducharme has to know I know his identity! Does he hope to barricade himself inside his bakery?

Ahead, Ducharme stumbled and cursed loudly, then tried to continue on in an ungainly limp.

Luc tackled him to the ground amidst the sounds of screams and the siren of the approaching Aix police. He handcuffed Ducharme and jerked him to an upright position. Ducharme instantly spat in his face and it took every ounce of strength Luc had not to backhand him.

"I knew that bitch would sic the cops on me!" Ducharme screamed, his eyes wild with fear and loathing. "She's trying to make them believe I killed Marine! I knew it!"

Luc wiped the spittle from his face and sat back on his heels. Ducharme was speaking to the crowd that had gathered around them.

The police car roared up onto the sidewalk and swiveled around the fountain of Roi René, coming to a screeching stop near Luc and Ducharme.

Three policemen got out. Luc recognized Sommet immediately.

"I have been assaulted!" Ducharme screamed to the police. "Arrest this maniac!"

Sommet looked at Ducharme and then at Luc.

"He attacked me in the alley on rue Manuel," Luc said.

"I did not attack him *or* the bitch!" Ducharme said. "I never saw them."

"I was with a female companion," Luc said.

Sommet gestured for his men to haul Ducharme up and into the back of the police car.

"Where are you taking me? I am innocent! I never touched Marine! Ask my daughter! She'll tell you I wasn't even at the bakery that night! I can prove it!"

Luc stood up and dusted off his trousers.

"Why is Ducharme not a suspect in his wife's murder?"

Sommet sneered at Luc. "This is an active investigation. I am not at liberty to discuss it."

Luc watched them manhandle Ducharme into the back of the car.

Something didn't feel right. Up to now Ducharme had not been a suspect in his wife's murder. The case notes Luc had read indicated there was no evidence linking him to the crime. The notes also said that his daughter Nicole had given him his alibi. And now he was saying he wasn't at the bakery that night.

So why would he assault us? Unless he was nervous that the police would turn their attention to him if White were released? It was a reasonable assumption. If White was innocent—threatening note or not—the wife-beating spouse would certainly be next in line on the list of suspects.

Luc looked at Sommet as the Aix detective lit a cigarette and waved the gathered crowd to disperse them.

Unless he was being protected in some way.

Was White arrested because he was American? A motion grabbed Luc's attention and he watched a young woman with two little French bull terriers walk under the street lights.

The dog. Jules thought the mysterious dog walker was important.

All joking aside, Luc thought, was it really believable that an investigating police officer would note the breed of dog but *not* take the man's name?

No. It was not.

"Brigadier Sommet," Luc said loudly. "I need to speak to the man who interviewed the eyewitness the night of Marine Ducharme's murder."

❈ ❈ ❈ ❈ ❈

Gone for good?

He *left*? Is that what she meant? He's *gone*?

I felt the shock and disappointment flood through me in sickening waves as I stepped back from the bakery.

So it was Raoul. All this time. Dammit! And he escaped!

How could I have been so slow? I'd actually spoken to him this very day. At the memory—and because I was feeling a little shaky after everything that had happened, I moved to sit on the bench across the street from the bakery.

I sat in the dark and took in a long breath.

Raoul was gone because I was too slow at putting all the pieces together.

I stared at the bakery and watched as the young woman inside moved about with the lantern until finally the front door opened again.

This time she had a flashlight and a jacket over her arm with her bag over her shoulder.

And she was holding the leash of a small black Labrador dog.

Cocoa.

My mind was in a whirl. This didn't make sense. Why would Raul leave and not take his dog?

I approached the woman and she turned with a worried look on her face until she saw it was me.

"Raoul didn't take his dog?" I asked, pointing to Cocoa.

It was impossible to understand what she said back to me. I heard the word *Raoul* and I understood *Cocoa*.

"Who dog?" I said pointing again to the dog. "*Qui* belongs to?"

She frowned. "*Je comprends pas*," she said, tugging on the leash to walk away.

"*Votre chien?*" I said, desperately trying another tact.

"*Non, non! Cocoa est le chien de Monsieur Bliss.*"
Cocoa belongs to Monsieur Bliss.

I'd jumped to the conclusion that Cocoa was Raoul's. And I was wrong.

Raoul hadn't been the mysterious eyewitness dog walker that night.

It was Albert Bliss.

Holy crap. *A. B.*

As all the pieces began to jump together I couldn't take my eyes off the dog.

The witness's dog was a small lab, like Cocoa. Nicole said a dog was in the alley barking at the time of the murder. Which is exactly what Cocoa does and exactly what she did that night because she didn't like to wait when her owner left her in an alley tied up while he went inside to murder someone.

I caught my breath. Except Bliss wasn't in Aix during the murder. Was he?

Unless that was a lie. Had anybody confirmed his alibi?

But Bliss didn't need to compete with Ducharme's. He had a flagship bakery opening in Nice in a few weeks!

Except there were other motives besides professional ones.

"Where...*ou es* Monsieur Bliss right now?" I asked, as the girl tried to push past me.

"And who is asking for me?"

I turned around to see Albert Bliss walking toward both of us, that big easy grin on his face and that twinkle in his eye. He was reaching for the dog leash.

I saw what happened next as if it were in slow motion. I saw his hand reaching for the leash and I saw the distinctive white strip of untanned flesh on his pinkie finger that indicated a ring was usually worn there.

A ring no doubt bearing the initials, A. B.

Albert Bliss.

"You killed Marine Ducharme," I blurted out.

23

To Catch a Falling Knife

Bliss looked over my shoulder at the girl, no doubt to confirm that she didn't understand what I'd said. Then he spoke to her and we both waited as the girl turned and walked off into the dark, her high heels shoes making that trademark echoing sound against the stone until they completely faded away.

Then he reached down to tousle Cocoa's ears before addressing me.

"You and who else think this nonsense?"

Oh, I could see where this was going and while a cold needle of fear went right up my backbone, I ignored it and managed to smile.

"The chief detective of the Aix police for one," I said, "who'll be here any minute to ask you the specifics of *this nonsense* as you put it. I know it was your ring, Monsieur Bliss, found in the caramel. And now I know that *that* was what you were really looking for the day I interrupted you at Ducharme's—not a caramel recipe. You were looking for the ring that came off when you killed Marine Ducharme."

"Very good," Bliss said amiably, his teeth flashing white around a smile that made my blood run cold.

"How did you know Elliott?" I asked.

"I didn't," he said, petting the dog. "Marine and I were at a party a few weeks back and she pointed him out to me as the American student screwing one of her employees." He looked at me. "So when I saw him leaving the bakery that night, I believed there must be more going on than she'd let on."

"Except that wasn't true," I said. "There was nothing between Madame Ducharme and Elliott."

He shrugged. "My bad, as you Americans say."

His off-hand attitude chilled me.

"But why Agnes?" I said impulsively. "Why kill *her*?"

You didn't have to be Jessica Fletcher to draw the connection between the owner of La Bouche being a big fat murderer and Agnes dying next to an empty bag of La Bouche pastries.

He shrugged again. "Simple. She saw me that night."

I thought he would say more. That's my excuse for why I didn't know what was coming next. I thought there would be more words.

It was possible I telegraphed my intention to run by looking in the direction that the girl had gone. Or that I was busy warming to the fact that I'd actually found the murderer and was mesmerized by all the supporting evidence stacking up so beautifully in my mind.

Whatever the reason I wasn't ready when he hit me.

His hand shot out and slapped me so hard I rocked back on my heels. I would've fallen but he lunged out and grabbed me by the throat with his other hand.

I felt my breath cut off like a knife slicing off my air. My hands flailed in the air as if that would get my breath back again.

I heard him laugh a low throaty chuckle. More of a growl, really.

And I knew I was dying. I couldn't breathe. The pressure of his fingers dug into my throat and my vision turned black, a sickening, dizzying blackness.

And then I heard a harsh gargle of a scream and all the colors of the rainbow came flowing back into my brain as I sank to the ground a second time that night, breathing in huge gulps of oxygen.

When I opened my eyes I was alone except for the little dog who was sitting so close to me, she was practically on top of me. I lifted a hand to touch her and when I did she turned to me and whined. Even in the dark I could see the blood on her mouth.

But when she turned to nuzzle my face, I could tell it wasn't her blood. I groaned and pulled her close to me. I couldn't tell which of us was trembling more. Suddenly I heard voices and I heard someone calling my name.

Luc.

I tried several times to call back but I didn't have the breath or the energy. That's when Cocoa started barking. Within seconds I heard the sounds of running feet getting closer.

"Jules!"

Luc knelt beside me, speaking French—none of which I understood—and ran his hands over me to see where I was hurt.

"I'm fine," I croaked, my throat suddenly on fire. "Albert Bliss killed Madame Ducharme. He tried to kill me." I put my hand to my throat. I knew it would be bruised tomorrow but now at least I *had* a tomorrow. "Cocoa saved me."

Luc turned and called out something in French to the two policemen who had just run up next to him.

171

They quickly turned and ran off and then without another word Luc scooped me up in his arms. I laid my head against his chest and closed my eyes.

"Luc?" I said softly.

"*Oui, chérie*?"

"Don't forget my dog, please."

24

Closing Ranks

If you can believe it, one week after that truly terrifying moment in my life I was sitting on an ancient stone patio drinking iced tea and marveling that I was still alive.

And not just alive but living in this amazing house on the outskirts of Chabanel.

A twelfth-century carriage house, *La Fleurette* sat on a small rise surrounded by fields, a weed-infested *potager* that showed promise and an ancient stonewall encircling a muddled garden behind the house. Honeysuckle and lavender ran riot on the perimeter of the small terrace where I now sat and lined the half-moon drive in front of the house.

It was old. Nearly falling down old. It had been vacant for years.

And it was perfect.

Both Neige and Camille, the two apartment building cats seemed to have adapted immediately to their change in situation. They sat now like stone sentinels on either side of the French doors which led into the back of the house, their eyes watching the bushes and tangled undergrowth for any hint that a mouse or vol might show itself.

As committed hunters and protectors of their turf, both clearly preferred the outdoor life to apartment living.

I have to say I felt much the same.

After all the excitement of capturing Albert Bliss who'd suffered a serious dog bite on his forearm and who did everyone a big favor by—I'm not sure you could call it *confessing* what with all the *you police are so stupide* ejaculations interspersed in his deposition— but let's just say boastfully confirmed that he'd killed Marine Ducharme.

He said it happened after he'd arrived early at her bakery for a planned assignation with Madame Ducharme only to see Elliott White leave her bakery in what he assumed was a romantic rendezvous.

While Bliss later realized he'd gotten the wrong end of the stick, at the time his fury at believing himself cuckolded by his lady love resulted in a spontaneous bath of hot caramel for poor Madame Ducharme—after he'd knocked her out with the caramel paddle— lost his signet ring in the process and put a word in the right ear that got Elliott arrested for the crime.

I stood up and stretched the kinks out of my back. From where I stood on the patio I could see over the walled garden to the vineyards and fields beyond. How Luc found this place and arranged things such that I would be able to live here, I have no idea. He promised he would tell me some day and I'm going to hold him to that.

"Jules, *avez-vous vu ces jolies tomates?*" Madame Becque came out of the house with a plate of sliced tomatoes in her hands which she placed on the table outside the door.

Oh, yeah, that's the other big change in my life. Madame Becque and her sister, Madame Cazaly are living with me now. While it had only been a week it was already working out great for everyone. The two old ladies needed someone to keep an eye on them and they, poor deluded souls, thought the same thing about me.

"I have no idea what it was you just said," I said to her, getting up to admire the tomatoes glistening with dressing and baked garlic. She wagged a finger at me and smiled before turning back to the kitchen.

Honestly, I'm pretty sure I'm getting the better part of the deal. Both *les soeurs* are amazing cooks and they know all the old ways about mending, housekeeping and most of all gardening. Already there were people dropping off goods like water, soap, wine and money in exchange for the Madame Twins' handiwork.

I only hope I can eventually bring something to the table half as useful.

The sharp sound of a barking dog heralded that Luc had arrived for dinner. He entered the back terrace through the garden gate which led to the road and beyond that to Chabanel.

I couldn't help but think how handsome he looked in the late summer light. Cocoa jumped up on him in greeting before Luc joined me on the back terrace and kissed me on both cheeks—something which still never failed to make me blush.

"Great guard dog you have there," Luc said wryly as he went to the outdoor sideboard to pour us both a glass of wine. "You look very beautiful this evening, Jules. You are recovered, yes?"

Cocoa dashed across the terrace and over the fence in search of imaginary rabbits or whatever devilish prey she thought was out there.

"I am recovered, yes," I said, taking the wine glass and touching my cheek where Bliss had hit me. It was no longer swollen and the bruise was almost completely faded. "I must say I really have to do a better job of putting all the pieces together *before* the bad guy is about to kill me."

Luc frowned. I know he didn't always understand my sense of humor.

"Perhaps we might hope that you will not put yourself in the way of any more bad guys?"

"Luc, we've talked about this. I can't quit. I think I might actually be good at it."

"And how lucrative are you finding it so far?"

"That's not fair. I've only had one real case."

But honestly he had a point. As grateful as both Jane and Glenn White were to have their son released from police custody—and they were bonkers with gratitude—as far as *financial* thanks not so much. Amid tears of gratitude Jane told me she would be on antidepressants if she could find them nowadays for the way they'd hired me *knowing that they had no way to pay me.*

That's right. They welched!

Turns out, I was right about the guilt I saw in them. They were *riddled* with guilt. Only it wasn't because they knew Elliott was the murderer or because they themselves had had a hand in Madame Ducharme's death.

It was because they knew they weren't going to be able to pay me.

When Elliott was released Glenn practically wept with shame and joy—if you can imagine such a combination—saying he and Jane had been nearly apoplectic they were so stressed over the whole situation.

So what was I going to do? Be a big person and tell them freeing Elliott for its own sake was what was important?

Yeah, right. So that's what I did.

The Madame Twins came out with trays of food—plates of several different kinds of cheese, shaved prosciutto and salami with large bowls of green and black olives—and scurried away to get table linens, napkins and silverware.

If I had to say they—like the cats—looked more alive it was because unlike at the apartment, here at *La Fleurette*, they bustled, they cleaned, they baked. They even sang.

When I'd come back to Chabanel last week they took me back with open arms and no questions asked.

Nah. I'm joking about the no questions thing. But I didn't have to worry about coming up with the answers. I just watched their shocked and appalled faces as Luc explained everything that had happened and in the end, they both threw their arms around me. With the exception of Madame C who hugged me but also slapped me upside the head. In her mind it was probably a Gallic love tap.

After that, when Luc surprised us with this amazing little farm, well, that was that. The old girls were only too happy to move out of the apartment which, it turned out, they didn't even own, and I was grateful to be somewhere I didn't have to worry about someone showing up and throwing me out of.

Luc went to examine the wood grill. Fortunately it wasn't an antique found on the property but one that Luc had brought over—from where I didn't know and didn't ask.

The fact that it fired up easily with only kindling and whatever sticks could be found in the surrounding woods was all I needed to know. He adjusted the grate over the low fire which was waiting for the marinated vegetables and chicken that the sisters would bring out any minute.

Before then, I had a few things I wanted to ask Luc about in private.

After Albert Bliss's arrest and Elliott's release, Luc and I'd spent a good portion of the last week debriefing on how and why the Bliss-Ducharme case had finally come together the way it did. The missed clues, the misread signs, the lost opportunities. I know I wished I'd asked better questions of Nicole and even Agnes.

Don't get me started on how the Aix police screwed up. But Luc assured me that he'd already pointed out to them all the ways they'd dropped the ball. And there were many.

From not grilling the young cadet who'd originally taken Bliss's eyewitness testimony that night but not his name, to neglecting to follow up on Bliss's alibi.

And oh yes, it turned out that Achiles Sommet and Felix Ducharme had gone to school together. *Quelle surprise* as the French like to say.

I thought Sommet should have lost his job over that but Luc only shrugged.

"I've been meaning to ask you how you knew to come to La Bouche that night?" I asked as I popped an olive into my mouth.

Luc sat down, stretching out his long legs. He looked very relaxed and very much at home on my terrace.

"I got to thinking about how you said it was hard to believe that the police did not get the name of the witness. The more I thought about it, the more I had to agree with you."

"I know what that must have cost you," I said teasingly.

He raised an eyebrow. "So after I talked with the man and he revealed that it was Albert Bliss that night in the alley with the dog..." Luc shrugged as if to say of course he then went to La Bouche to find Bliss.

"So did the cop hold back Bliss's name because he knew him personally?" I asked.

"Not really. His family had of course bought its bread from La Bouche for years so the cadet recognized Bliss but when Bliss asked him to take his information but keep his name out of it, the young man complied."

"And his superiors accepted that?"

"Sommet accepted that the young policeman failed to get the witness's name. The cadet was even punished for the oversight. Quite severely in fact."

"So why did he do it?"

"Bliss offered him free *profiteroles* for life."

I shook my head in wonder. "Wow. That would be pretty tempting for anyone. But for a *Frenchman*?"

"What about your own reward?" Luc said, his eyes twinkling. "Free *baguettes* for as long as you are in France?"

Several of the other *boulangeries* in Aix had gotten together and offered to give me a baguette a day for pretty much life for helping to find Marine Ducharme's killer.

Between you and me, I think it was because I single-handedly eliminated two of their biggest competitors.

"Yeah," I said, "and that would be great if the bakeries weren't all in Aix. Am I really supposed to ride my bike to Aix every morning to collect? Don't answer that, you sadist. Most *normal* people would rather starve than do something so mad."

Luc laughed. "Well, you better not let *les soeurs* hear about the reward," he said. "They will be pushing you out the door and handing you your bike helmet."

"Aw, that's sweet that you think they'd care about a bike helmet."

All the other loose ends had been tidily plaited and snipped off. It turned out that Agnes had gone to Bliss for a job at La Bouche and when he wasn't interested, she revealed that she'd seen him leave the bakery that night when she'd come to try to have a word with Nicole.

She offered to go to the police with her information if Bliss didn't see fit to employ her as his newest pastry chef—a position that honestly, most people agreed she was hardly qualified for.

Blackmail is certainly as good a reason to kill as any other—or at least that's what Bliss thought. And after you've done it once, I guess the second time is easier.

After assaulting a police officer, Felix Ducharme was strongly urged by the Aix police force to relocate to the north which he did with much bad grace. I was surprised that Luc didn't press the issue but maybe they were running out of places to stick criminals in the apocalypse.

Oh, and the signet ring and Barry's check along with my favorite Kate Spade bag were all found at Ducharme's bakery leading me to believe that the night Felix attacked me and Luc had not been the first time the guy had followed me. Ducharme seemed to think— absolutely correctly—that I was trying to stick the murder rap on *him* and he'd become obsessed with stopping me somehow.

Nicole, who it turned out had in fact inherited the bakery and who—in a shocking revelation—admitted that she didn't eat carbs, was in the process of selling the bakery to move to Paris.

Very tidy indeed.

As for La Bouche, it was closed permanently, and many think that is the real disaster in this whole mess.

They truly made the most amazing almond croissants.

The sounds of the sisters talking and laughing in the kitchen warned both me and Luc that they would be joining us at any moment.

Cocoa jumped over the stone wall and ran to me where she lay panting at my feet, her tongue lolling, her eyes glued adoringly on me.

I put my hand on her head and I swear she closed her eyes in mute pleasure.

I never had a dog growing up.

I'm pretty sure I'll never be without one again.

"So before *les soeurs* come," Luc said, tousling Cocoa's ears. "Tell me again how you knew it was Bliss?"

"I didn't," I admitted. "Until he took Cocoa's leash, all I knew was that it had to be a baker or window designer—probably Raoul—because of the cherries placement."

Whereas the Aix cops saw the cherries and the flour dumped on Madame Ducharme as simply signs of rage—and one more reason why they thought the killer must be American and not French—I couldn't help think *what murderer would stop to decorate his murder victim?* Who would do that except someone used to decorating everything they created for show and special display?

Luc raised an eyebrow and I was struck—as I often am at odd times—by how effortlessly handsome he was. *The truly gorgeous ones usually don't even know it.* After everything we'd been through, I'd found a moment in the last few days to tell Luc that he was not allowed to disappear on me again. But honestly, something in the way he looked at me now made me believe that that would not be a problem.

"Jules? The cherries?" Luc prompted me.

"Oh, right, sorry. So I asked myself, what murderer *kills* someone and then positions *cherries* on her head? I mean, who would *do* that? The answer of course was— either a real psycho..."

"Or a professional pastry chef," Luc said with a grin.

"*Exactement!*"

"Your French is improving, *chérie*."

"It's the only word I know so far."

"Well, it is a good one."

"So are you, Chief DeBray," I said feeling a glow right down to my toes that had nothing at all to do with the wine or the gently dropping summer sun.

To see what happens next to Jules and life in post-apocalyptic France, be sure and check out Book 3 in the *Stranded in Provence* Mystery series, *Accent on Murder*.

ABOUT THE AUTHOR

Susan Kiernan-Lewis lives in Ponte Vedra, Florida and writes mysteries and romantic suspense. Like many authors, Susan depends on the reviews and word of mouth referrals of her readers. If you enjoyed *Crime and Croissants* please consider leaving a review saying so on Amazon.com, Barnesandnoble.com or Goodreads.com. Check out Susan's website at susankiernanlewis.com and feel free to contact her at sanmarcopress@me.com.

30034913R00115

Made in the USA
San Bernardino, CA
21 March 2019